The Mouse that Roared

This is a lively collection of animal fables – all new and all refreshingly and simply told.

There are twenty stories in all and they are wide-ranging in their appeal. There are funny ones like 'The Stew', where the animals quarrel over the largest share – and end with none at all. There is the sad story of Jenny Wren and her beautiful nest. The title story – 'The mouse that roared' – is a humorous warning to those who get too big for their boots, while 'The Kite' tells how Fox makes a dream come true.

Ray Jones works in the education department of a zoo. As he works he hears many sounds – the roaring of lions, the whooping of gibbons, the honking of sealions, and the excited chatter of young visitors – which have provided him with the inspiration for the delightful characters in this book.

Ray Jones

The Mouse that Roared
and other animal fables

illustrated by Shirley Felts

Piccolo Books
in association with Heinemann

First published 1979 by William Heinemann Ltd
This Piccolo edition published 1981 by Pan Books Ltd,
Cavaye Place, London SW10 9PG
in association with William Heinemann Ltd
2nd Printing 1982
© Ray Jones 1979
illustrations © Shirley Felts 1979
ISBN 0 330 26383 8
Set in Great Britain by
Northumberland Press Ltd, Gateshead, Tyne and Wear
Printed and bound by
Richard Clay (The Chaucer Press) Ltd, Bungay, Suffolk

Contents

The mouse that roared

As Lion stalked the plains and jungles all the other animals ran away and hid themselves.

'How wonderful it must be,' said Mouse to himself, 'to be like Lion, to walk the earth like a king, respected and feared by all beasts, afraid of nothing.' He sighed to himself, 'How I would love to be like Lion.'

Just then Lion roared, *ahhhggraaahhh*. Mouse trembled with fear and ran down the nearest hole in the ground.

At last Mouse stopped trembling and came out of his hole. 'It's not fair,' he grumbled. 'Even when Lion is miles away and can't harm me, I am terrified and hide away like a coward.'

Mouse lay down in the hot sun but he couldn't sleep. He kept thinking about Lion. Why was it they were all terrified of him? He wasn't the largest beast. Elephant was much bigger. So were Giraffe and Hippo but no one was afraid of them. He wasn't the most ferocious, Rhino was much worse. When Rhino had one of his rages the whole jungle shook and he rushed about in a frenzy, crushing anything that was in his way. But most of the time the other animals just laughed at him, he was such a clumsy fellow and so ugly. No, there was something special about Lion. What was it?

Just then Lion roared again, a quiet roar from far away, a roar of contentment as though he had eaten a good meal and was now settling down to a comfortable snooze. Again Mouse trembled and his little heart beat pit-a-pat, pit-a-pat, even though he knew there was nothing to be afraid of.

Mouse lay in the hot sun for a long time thinking and at last he decided that he knew the secret of Lion's power. It was his roar, that terrible *ahhhggraaahhh*. It was quiet at first, rumbling and grumbling in his throat, and then as Lion opened his great jaws, it came pouring out, echoing from the trees and making even the leaves shake with fear. Yes, of course, that was what it was. No other beast had a roar like it. Now he had solved the problem, Mouse turned over and went to sleep.

Mouse gave a lot of thought to Lion and his terrible roar. 'If only I could roar like that,' he said to himself, 'all the other beasts would be frightened of me. They would respect *me* just as they respect Lion.'

He began to practise roaring. He tried to imitate that menacing rumble in his throat that Lion did so well, but all that came out was a gurgling squeak. He tried again. He placed his feet firmly on the ground, glared up at the heavens, opened his jaws wide and gave another roar. *Gr-r-r-r-argle-argle-argle*, came the sound. It was better, but nothing like a roar. Caterpillar, who was having a little nap, was woken up by the noise and was so startled that he fell off his leaf.

Mouse was encouraged by this. 'If I can frighten Caterpillar,' he said, 'I can frighten the other beasts. I will practise again and again until I sound just like Lion.'

Mouse practised and each day his roar grew more like that of Lion. Soon he could manage that rumbling, grumbling sound quite well and when he opened his mouth wide and let out the roar the blades of grass nearby gently trembled. Some of the little creatures stopped nibbling grass and leaves for a few moments and looked up in surprise, but when they saw that it was only Mouse who was making the strange noise they carried on eating and ignored him.

'It's no good,' said Mouse one day after he had been practising his roar for several weeks, 'I shall never be able to roar like Lion.' His throat was sore with the effort he had been making. 'I'm too small, that's the trouble, and my roar is not loud enough. If I were bigger I could roar just like Lion, I know I could, and all the beasts of the jungle would fear and respect me,' and he cried tears of disappointment.

Mouse was a determined creature and he continued to practise his roar. One day he was practising when it began to rain. He looked round for somewhere to shelter and saw a hollow tree. He jumped into the tree through a small hole. The rain showed no sign of stopping so Mouse decided to practise his roar inside the tree.

Grr-aahhhhrrraaahhh. He roared just like he always did, but this time it was quite different. The sound was magnified by the hollow tree. It was a thousand times louder than he had ever roared before. Mouse fell over with surprise at the terrible noise as it echoed and re-echoed up the hollow tree. It was like Lion's roar. Just like Lion's roar. Had *he*, Mouse, made that terrible roar? He couldn't believe it. He decided to try again. He braced his feet firmly and looked up into the dark of the hollow tree. He began quietly with the menacing rumble sound, *grrrr*. The tree began to

shake. Now he opened his mouth wide and let the roar come pouring out. *Arrrggghhhh!* Again. *Aaarrrggg-hhhh! Aaarrrrggggghhhhhh!* His eyes bulged and tears ran down his cheeks with the effort, but it was worth it. The sound was wonderful, just like Lion's roar.

Mouse popped his head out of the hole in the hollow tree. He saw a very strange sight. Beasts were running in all directions. Hippo pounded past searching for a pool; Giraffe galloped this way and that looking for somewhere to hide; Wildebeest came past and Deer and Waterbuffalo and Zebra. Round and round they ran in a panic looking for hiding places and there was terror in their eyes. More and more beasts came past. The jungle shook as their hooves thundered on the ground. Monkeys chattered and shrieked with terror and flew to the tops of the trees. Birds and butterflies fluttered hither and thither.

Mouse was astonished. He had never seen the beasts of the jungle so frightened before. What could have caused it? Only the roar of Lion caused that much fear. And then the truth occurred to him. It wasn't Lion's roar that had caused the fear. It was *his* roar. *His* roar. He laughed to himself. At last he had won the fear and respect of the other animals. He did a little jig for joy and then lay down inside the hollow tree and went to sleep, for he was feeling tired after his roaring.

Mouse made his home inside the hollow tree. Each day he roared. He loved to see the panic he caused among the beasts as they ran round and round looking for somewhere to hide, for they all thought he was Lion. When one of them came near the hollow tree, minding his own business, nibbling plants or leaves, Mouse would give out a terribly frightening roar that would set the poor creature trembling with terror. Mouse would look out of the hole in the tree as it went scampering away and would laugh until the tears ran down his cheeks.

One day poor Buffalo was so terrified by Mouse's roar that when he tried to run away his legs wouldn't take him and he fell over. Mouse popped his head out of the hole to have a good laugh, and Buffalo saw him.

'Was that you who roared?' asked Buffalo.

'Tee hee hee,' laughed Mouse. 'Tee hee hee hee hee hee hee.'

Buffalo was angry. He rushed at Mouse and Mouse had to jump back quickly into the tree to avoid Buffalo's terrible horns. Buffalo took out his anger on the tree. He charged at it again and again, but the tree was large and he did it no harm. He just gave himself a headache.

Mouse laughed again. Now his laughter was magnified by the hollow tree and it echoed and re-echoed throughout the jungle.

Parrot ventured out to see what was happening.

'What's going on?' she said.

'It's Mouse,' said Buffalo, and he explained to Parrot how Mouse was imitating Lion's roar.

Parrot was a very talkative bird and she told everyone about the hollow tree and how it was Mouse and not Lion who had been frightening them to death during the past few weeks. They all felt foolish. To think that it was Mouse, timid little Mouse, they had all been running away from in terror, and not Lion at all! They were very annoyed.

Parrot even told Lion. Lion gave a terrifying roar of anger and she had to fly away to the treetops for safety. Eventually he calmed down. Parrot flew towards the hollow tree and Lion followed her.

Lion put his eye to the hole in the hollow tree. Inside Mouse was cowering in terror.

'Have you been pretending to be me?' demanded Lion in his deep voice. 'Have you? Eh? Have you been pretending to be Mighty Lion, King of the Jungle?'

Mouse was too frightened to lie. He nodded his head. Lion put his mouth to the hollow tree and let out a roar. AAARRRGGGHHHHHHHHH ... Mouse could feel the hot breath on him and he trembled. Deep down in his little Mouse's soul he trembled. How he wished he had never pretended to be Lion.

Lion roared again. AAARRRGGGHHHHHH-HH ... AAARRRGGGHHHHHHHHH ... AAA-RRRGGGHHHHHHHHH ... The sound magnified inside the hollow tree. It echoed over the jungle like a volcano erupting. Mouse thought his eardrums would burst with the noise. The whole jungle shook. All the birds and beasts hid deep in their hiding places. Again and again Lion roared. He began to claw at the hollow tree. Lumps of bark flew off it, but he couldn't get at Mouse for the tree was too big and strong. He went away, snarling with rage and disappointment.

Mouse never pretended to be Lion again. He realized that Lion was more than just a roar. He was Mighty Lion, King of the Jungle, respected and feared by all beasts; whilst he was Mouse, respected and feared by none. This was the way things were and the way things would always be. He knew that if he ever roared again Lion would come and catch him: he would breathe his hot breath over him and crush him between his great teeth. Mouse loved life too much to risk that. And so he made up his mind to be happy as himself, Mouse.

The fox and the greedy duck

The winter was hard and the world was covered with snow. The birds and beasts had very little to eat. Mr and Mrs Fox, who usually ate fat rabbits and plump pheasants for their supper, were making a meal of stale crusts of bread which Mrs Fox had collected from dustbins.

'I hate bread,' said Fox as he nibbled unhappily at a crust.

'So do I,' said his wife, 'but if we don't eat this we shall starve, for there is nothing else.'

Some ducks saw Mr and Mrs Fox eating and they flew down. 'Quack!' they said. 'Quack, quack, quack! We are hungry; starving. Please give us something to eat.'

Fox threw them a crust. One of the ducks, the biggest and fattest, fell upon a crust and gulped it down, not leaving a crumb for any of the others.

Fox threw another crust. Again the fat duck grabbed it and swallowed it, knocking down the other ducks who tried to get it first.

'I didn't collect those crusts so that you could feed those ducks with them,' said Mrs Fox. 'If you don't want them, leave them for me. I will eat them.'

Fox ignored her. He threw another crust to the

ducks. Again the fat duck pushed aside the others and grabbed the crust.

Fox threw another crust, which went straight to the fat duck. He gobbled it down, not giving the others a chance.

Mrs Fox was angry with Fox. She had spent all day collecting the crusts, risking the dangers of savage dogs and men with stones, and here was her stupid husband giving them to these stupid ducks. 'If you must give away your supper,' she said, 'at least share it amongst the ducks equally. Don't give it all to that big greedy one.'

Fox ignored what his wife said. He threw another

crust to the fat duck, and another, and another, until his supper had all gone. Then he grabbed his wife's crusts and began to throw those to the ducks too, making sure that they all went to the fat duck. Mrs Fox was very annoyed. She got up in a huff and ran off. She would never speak to her husband again. From now on he could collect his own supper. To think she had once thought him clever – sly, even. How foolish she had been.

Fox threw his wife's crusts to the ducks one after the other. The fat duck, who was now stronger and greedier than ever, gulped down every one, not giving the others a chance.

Fox now had nothing left to give the ducks. He got up to go. The ducks, who didn't really trust Fox, flew away – all except the fat duck who had eaten so much bread that he couldn't fly. He flapped his wings hard, but all in vain, his body was too heavy to rise up from the ground. Fox walked up to him and screwed his neck.

'Yow-ow-ow! Ow-ow!' howled Fox, and his voice rang loud and triumphant in the moonlit sky. Mrs Fox heard him in her lair. What was he howling for, she wondered? She ran to find out.

Fox held up the fat, greedy duck to show his wife. 'I've caught our supper,' he said.

Mr and Mrs Fox shared the fat duck between them. 'You are very clever, Mr Fox,' said Mrs Fox to her husband, 'I always knew you were.' Fox said nothing. He brushed away some feathers from his greasy chops and smiled slyly at his wife, then he lay down to sleep.

The stew

'I am tired of eating chicken,' said Fox. 'Chicken, chicken, all I ever eat is chicken.'

'And I am tired of eating carrots,' said Hare.

'And I of potatoes,' said Badger.

'And I of cabbages,' said Rabbit.

'And I of truffles,' said Mole.

'And I of eggs,' said Weasel.

'Is there nothing different we could eat?' said Stoat.

'How about a nice stew?' said Shrew.

'A very good idea,' said Otter. 'We could get Dog and Cat to help us. They are sure to know how to make a stew.'

And so they all agreed to make a stew.

Dog collected fuel and kindled a fire.

Cat brought the pot and the salt and pepper.

Otter fetched the water.

Shrew brought tasty herbs and spices.

Stoat made the dumplings.

Weasel brought eggs.

Mole brought truffles.

Rabbit brought cabbages.

Badger brought potatoes.

Hare brought carrot.

Fox brought chickens.

Cat cut up the ingredients and dropped them into

the water. Dog blew the fire to make it hot. The others sat and watched. Occasionally Cat would stir the stew and taste it to see if it required more salt or pepper. It smelled delicious. Their noses twitched. How they looked forward to eating that stew. The meat and vege-tables and the herbs and spices slowly cooked, and the flavours, mingled together. Never had a stew smelled as beautiful as that stew. The aroma crawled and crept, and slunk and slithered, and spread and sprawled throughout the wood. The leaves on the trees bent down to sniff at it and the blades of grass gulped the aroma down.

Fox, Hare, Badger, Rabbit, Mole, Weasel, Stoat, Shrew, Otter, Dog and Cat trembled and twitched and fidgeted and fumbled and yawned and yapped and grunted and growled and licked their hungry chops. The stew bubbled away upon the fire.

'I will have the largest share,' said Fox.

'No I will have the largest share,' said Hare.

'No I,' said Badger.

'I,' said Rabbit.

'I,' said Mole.

'I, I, I, I, I, I,' said Weasel, Stoat, Shrew, Otter, Dog, and Cat.

'The chickens are the most important ingredient in the stew,' said Fox, 'and therefore I should get the largest share.'

'Nonsense!' said Hare, 'The carrots are the most important ingredient.'

'The potatoes!' said Badger.

'Cabbage!' said Rabbit.

'Truffles!' said Mole.

'Eggs!'

'Dumplings!'

'Water!'

'I made the fire,' said Dog. 'You can't make a stew without fire.'

'And I made the stew,' said Cat, 'so obviously I should get the largest share.'

'Rubbish!' said Fox, Hare, Badger, Rabbit, Mole, Weasel, Stoat, Shrew, Otter and Dog.

The stew bubbled away upon the fire.

'Chickens give the stew its body,' said Fox.

'And so do potatoes,' said Badger.

'And eggs.'

'And dumplings.'

'Rubbish!'

'Piffle!'

'Poppycock!'

'Carrots give it flavour,' said Hare.

'And cabbages.'

'And truffles.'

'And herbs and spices.'

'Poppycock!'

'Piffle!'

'Rubbish!'

The stew bubbled away upon the fire.

'You shall not have the largest share.'

'Yes I will.'

'No.'

'Yes.'

'No.'

'No.'

'No.'

The stew bubbled away upon the fire.

'You're a greedy beast!'

'You're a black villain!'

'A rogue!'

'A thief!'

'An idiot!'

'A fool!'

'A coward!'

'A scoundrel!'

The stew stopped bubbling upon the fire. No one noticed.

'I will teach you a lesson,' said Fox, and he struck Hare. Badger struck Fox. Rabbit struck Badger. Mole struck Rabbit. Weasel struck Mole. Stoat struck Weasel. Shrew struck Stoat. Otter struck Shrew. Dog struck Otter. Cat struck Dog.

'The stew!' shrieked the leaves and the grass. 'It's burning!'

The animals stopped fighting. The water in the stew had boiled away. Black smoke was pouring out of the pot. The stew was ruined.

'My chickens!' cried Fox.

'My carrots!' cried Hare.

'My potatoes!' cried Badger.

'My cabbages!' cried Rabbit.

'My truffles!' cried Mole.

'My eggs!' cried Weasel.

'My herbs and spices!' cried Shrew.

'Our beautiful stew!' cried Otter, Dog and Cat.

They emptied the burnt stew upon the ground and walked away into the wood, vowing never to make any more stew.

The rain came and washed away the burnt stew. It washed it deep into the ground. A thistle grew upon the ground and everyone who went that way pricked himself upon the thistle, but none of them knew anything about the stew.

Owl and Magpie

Owl, miserable Owl, perched on the bough of a tree. Magpie, cheerful Magpie, flew down and perched next to him.

'Hallo, Owl!' said Magpie. 'How are you old chap?'

Owl said nothing. He just stared miserably in front of him.

'Tell me, Owl,' said Magpie, not the least put out because Owl hadn't spoken to him, 'why are you always so miserable?'

Owl turned his head and looked sadly at Magpie, 'Because nobody likes me,' he said.

'And why does nobody like you!'

'Because I'm so miserable,' said Owl. 'Tell me Magpie,' went on Owl, 'why are you always cheerful?'

'Because everybody likes me,' said Magpie.

'And why does everybody like you?'

'Because I'm so cheerful,' said Magpie, and he flew away, leaving Owl on the bough of the tree staring miserably in front of him.

Mighty Lion and Tiger

Grrahh-h-h-h roared Lion with a mighty roar, 'I am the King of Beasts, Lion All Powerful.' And to prove his point he ate two zebra and a water-buffalo.

Grrraaah-h-h-h-h-h-h roared Tiger, with an even more powerful roar. 'I am the Emperor of Beasts, Tiger Almighty Powerful.' And to prove that he was more powerful than Lion he ate five cows and two red deer.

Grrraaaa-a-h-h-h-h-h-h roared Lion, 'How dare you! I am noble Lion. I am more powerful than you by far. All creatures are afraid of me.' And to make them more afraid he roared again and then ate ten giraffe and four wildebeest.

Grrrraaaaa-a-a-a-a-h-h-h-h roared Tiger, 'Nonsense! I am terrible Tiger. All the beasts of the earth tremble when I am near.' *Grrrrraaaa-a-a-a-a-h-h-h-h* and he ate up all the sheep, wolves, foxes and elephants.

GRRRRRAAAA-A-A-A-A-A-H-H-H roared Lion, now fuming with anger. 'You have the audacity to challenge the power of great Lion! I will show you that I am the greatest beast the world has ever known.'

G-R-R-R-R-R-A-A-A-A-A-A-H-H-H-H and he ate up all the pigs, camels, rhinos and hippos.

GRRR-R-R-R-R-A-A-A-A-A-A-H-H-H roared Tiger.

GRRR-R-R-R-R-A-A-A-A-A-A-A-H-H-H-H-H roared Lion.

The two great beasts ate up all the animals of the earth, the fishes of the sea and the birds of the air. There were now just the two of them left. So big and mighty were they that Lion now straddled one half of the world and Tiger the other.

Grrraaahhh, roared Lion now too gorged to roar as loudly as he once had roared, 'Can't you see now that I am the most powerful of all beasts?'

Grrraaahhh, roared Tiger, as gorged as Lion, 'It is obvious to all but a fool that I am the greatest.'

Grrraaahhh, spluttered Lion, 'Impertinent wretch. I will show you who is the greatest. I will eat you up.'

Grrraaahhh, coughed Tiger. 'Don't make me laugh. I will now make a snack of *you*.'

The two huge beasts opened their great jaws, each to eat up the other. But, so big was Tiger that Lion couldn't open his mouth wide enough, and so big was Lion that Tiger couldn't open his mouth wide enough either.

Aaaaahhhh, cried Lion, opening his mouth wider and wider and wider.

Aaaaahhhh, cried Tiger, opening his mouth wider still.

Suddenly there was a click. Lion's jaw had stuck; it was dislocated. Another click. Tiger had dislocated his jaw too.

Both beasts stood facing one another with mouths wide open and neither could shut them. Still, anger and hatred glinted in their eyes.

Suddenly, there was the sound of roaring, barking, mooing, trumpeting, squeaking and shrieking, getting louder and louder, like the coming of a great thunder storm, and from the jaws of Lion and Tiger there ran, flew, crawled and swam all the beasts, birds and fishes of the earth. They ate up Lion and Tiger, their flesh, organs and bones, until there was nothing left of them. Not even a *grrraaahhh* – a little roar.

The big fight

It was spring. Fox took in deep gulps of the clean, warm air. He yawned and stretched all his limbs. 'I feel marvellous,' he said. 'I am the greatest of all animals. I could fight any other creature in the wood. I am the cleverest, fittest, fastest, strongest of animals. Yes, indeed, I am the greatest.'

'Do you think you could fight Badger?' said Stoat, who happened to be passing and had heard what Fox said.

'Yes of course,' said Fox.

'And beat him?' asked Stoat.

'Easily,' yawned Fox and he lay down to have a little nap.

Stoat smiled to himself a crafty smile and hurried off to see Badger.

Badger was asleep when Stoat arrived, 'What do you want?' he growled bad temperedly, as Stoat poked him in the ribs to wake him up.

'I do apologize for waking you Badger,' said Stoat in his oiliest voice, 'but it's Fox, he says he's going to fight you.'

'What!' growled Badger, who didn't like Fox. He thought he was far too clever for his own good.

'He says he will beat you easily. He says he is the greatest animal in all the wood. He says he is the strongest, the fittest, the fastest ...'

'What!' bellowed Badger again. 'The impudent bounder, I'll bury him.' He got up and went towards the door.

'No, no, dear Badger,' said Stoat in his soothing voice. 'Don't go now. That is just what Fox wants. He is such a sly fellow. He is probably lying in wait for you with his cousins. They will jump out on you and ...'

'I'll bury them *all*,' bellowed Badger.

'No, no, no, Badger,' said Stoat. 'No, you must leave matters to me. I will see that a proper fight is arranged and that Fox doesn't cheat.'

Badger grunted, turned over, and went back to sleep. Stoat smiled his crafty smile and left Badger. He rubbed his hands together with glee as he skipped through the wood to see his friend Weasel. Stoat and Weasel had a long chat.

'Ah, my dear friend Fox,' said Weasel, who just happened to be passing Fox's home next morning. 'That wicked fellow Badger is saying some terrible things about you. I happened to bump into him yesterday and he said he was going to bury you. He said you were a loud-mouthed fool who couldn't fight his way through a light mist. He said that a flea doing a tap-dance on his nose would hurt him more than anything you could do to him. He said ...'

But Fox wasn't listening. He was pacing up and down in a terrible temper.

'How ... how ... how ... how ...' he said. And 'I'll ... I'll ... I'll ... I'll ...'

'Calm down dear Fox,' said Weasel. 'You'll do yourself a mischief.'

'How *dare* he say things like that about me!' shrieked Fox, snarling and baring his teeth. 'I'll murder him. I'll tear him limb from limb. The big bully I'll ... I'll ... I'll ...'

'Yes I'm sure you will Fox,' said Weasel, grinning a sly grin, 'I'm sure you will. Leave it to me and you shall. A fight must be arranged between you and Badger. But it must be a proper fight. Badger mustn't be allowed to cheat. I'll go and see my friend Stoat and we will arrange it.'

'Fox and Badger are going to fight.'

'Badger and Fox ...'

'A fight!'

'A fight!'

'A fight!'

The word spread through the wood like a fire, fanned by Stoat and Weasel. It ran and leapt and flew and blazed through the wood. A fight. Fox and Badger. Three weeks next Thursday. Grasshopper Glade. Get there early. Have a good seat. Everyone heard it with excitement. It went from Weasel to Squirrel to Hare to Otter to Vole; and from Stoat to Owl to Rabbit to Mouse to Mole and then to all their relations.

The creatures of the wood began to gather in Grasshopper Glade. They arrived two days before the fight was due to be fought. The animals came, and the birds, and the reptiles, and the insects. Stoat and Weasel had roped off a square in the middle of the glade and the creatures squabbled and fought among themselves to get places at the front where they would have a good view of the fight. Few of them had remembered to bring anything to eat. Luckily Stoat and his relatives had prepared sandwiches, hot dogs, roast chickens, hamburgers, and boiled lobsters which they sold to the creatures at very high prices. They all grumbled at paying more than the food was worth, but they paid it all the same for they didn't want to leave their places in order to fetch food. They knew that if they did someone would steal them.

Weasel and his relatives had stalls with bottles of lemonade, ice creams, lollipops, bottles of wine and beer and packets of nuts and chocolates. These also they sold at high prices and, although they grumbled, the creatures bought them.

They chattered among themselves as they waited impatiently for the fight to begin; they talked about only one thing – the fight, and who was going to win. Some thought that Fox would win with ease, others that Badger would win without difficulty. Others that it would be a very close thing and that either of the two might win or that it might even be a draw.

'Fox will mince Badger,' said Hare. 'He will be so fast that he will chop Badger into tiny pieces and Badger won't even see him.'

'Stuff and nonsense,' said Mole. 'Nothing Fox can do will hurt Badger. He might just as well try to fight an oak tree. Badger is so strong that he will need to hit Fox only once and Fox will need a coffin.'

'You,' said Hare, giving Mole a painful dig in the chest, 'don't,' giving him another dig, 'know,' dig, 'anything,' dig, 'about,' dig, 'fighting.'

'I know more about fighting,' said Mole, poking Hare eleven times with five sharp claws, 'than you will ever know.' And to emphasize his point he poked him ten more times.

At this Hare got to his feet, his face red with anger and began to pummel Mole with his fists. Mole hit Hare in the stomach with his head. Luckily Stoat came and stood in between them otherwise there would have been a fight there and then.

'Animals, animals, please,' said Stoat. 'There's no need to fight. Leave the fighting to Fox and Badger. Why not have a little bet instead. Hare, will you bet two pounds on Fox to beat Badger?'

'Five!' said Hare.

'And Mole, will you bet five pounds on Badger to beat Fox?' said Stoat.

'Ten!' said Mole.

Stoat took Hare and Mole's money.

'Anybody else to bet on Fox?' said Stoat to the crowd.

'Five pounds,' said one.

'Ten pounds,' said another.

'Fifteen.'

'And Badger?'

'Ten pounds.'

'Fifteen.'

'Twenty.'

Stoat took all their money, smiling his crafty smile. The whole glade buzzed with excitement and anticipation as they waited for Fox and Badger to appear. But they didn't appear. The crowd grew restless Stoat and Weasel leapt into the ring. 'Friends,' said

Stoat, waiting for the murmuring to die down, 'there is not much longer to wait before those two fantastic fighters of the forest – Fox,' there were cheers from the crowd, 'and Badger,' counter cheers, 'will come into the ring to take part in the event you have all been waiting for – the great fight.' A huge cheer from the whole crowd.

'I have been watching my friend Badger in training and I can assure you he is in fine shape. He is strong and fast. I think he will win the fight and become champion of the wood.' Stoat's words were drowned by cheers and boos from the crowd. Weasel began to speak.

'Friends! Friends! Friends!' he yelled, gradually making himself heard above the din. 'I can understand your indignation at what friend Stoat has said. I have just come from friend Fox and I can assure you he has never been fitter than he is now. He is so fast that his blows travel like streaks of lightning. I believe he will pulverize Badger. I believe *he* will become the champion of the wood.' There were more boos and cheers and whistles.

Stoat and Weasel kept the crowd in a state of bubbling excitement. First Stoat gave a list of all the insulting things he said he had heard Fox say about Badger and all the terrible things he said he was going to do to Badger. Then Weasel told the crowd what *he* said he had heard Badger say about Fox and what Badger was going to do to Fox. Between them they kept the crowd deliriously happy. Then Weasel showed them a copy of a book he had written all about the fight, listing the strengths and weaknesses of Fox and Badger; giving their exact ages, their weights, heights, lengths, colour of eyes, what time they went to bed, what time they got up, what food they ate, how they trained for the fight, what their hobbies were – in short, everything it was possible to know about them. 'Would any of you like to buy a copy of this book? I have a limited number of copies for sale at fifty pence each. The first ones to put their hands up will get them.'

Eagerly the hands went up, hundreds of them. Weasel produced hundred of copies of the book and he and his relatives went among the crowd distributing them and collecting the money. There were more than enough to go round. Eagerly they read the books from cover to cover.

Fox and Badger still hadn't appeared. It grew dusk in Grasshopper Glade. Some of the creatures fell asleep. Some, tired of talking, became silent. Others kept up the chatter, trying to keep alive the mood of excitement.

Night descended upon the glade. The wood grew silent. Eyelids fell over tired eyes. All the creatures were asleep. Still Fox and Badger had not appeared.

And now I must let you into a little secret. There were two creatures who knew nothing about the big fight. At least they had known something about it originally, but now they had forgotten and no one had bothered to remind them. These were Fox and Badger. Each was about his own business and had forgotten the existence of the other. Fox had quietly left the wood to visit a nearby farm. He was inspecting a new consignment of chickens that had just arrived with a view to acquiring some of them. Badger was in a deep sleep that would last for another five days at least, and it would be woe betide anyone who tried to rouse him from it.

The morning light crept through the wood. It quietly flooded Grasshopper Glade, bathing the creatures asleep there. They stretched their limbs and yawned, wondering what they were doing in Grasshopper Glade.

'Where is Stoat?' asked Rabbit, looking round the glade.

'And Weasel?' said Otter.

They had both gone and so had all their relatives, and so had the ropes that had formed the square in which Fox and Badger were to have fought. Slowly the truth dawned.

'Perhaps,' said Mouse, 'Badger and Fox had their fight while we were asleep.'

'Yes,' said Squirrel, 'perhaps they did.'

But they all knew different. They knew there had been no fight. Stoat and Weasel had tricked them. They had lured them to Grasshopper Glade in order to take their money off them.

At first the creatures felt angry with Stoat and Weasel for tricking them. Then they felt angry with themselves for allowing themselves to be tricked so easily. Then they just felt foolish. Slowly they drifted out of Grasshopper Glade and back to their homes.

'I don't know what I shall tell my wife and friends when I get home,' said Hare, his hands thrust deep into his empty pockets.

'Neither do I,' said Mole.

'I shall look a right fool having to admit that I have come so far and spent so much to see a fight that never took place. My wife will lock me out of the house and my friends will all laugh at me.'

'I know exactly how you feel,' said Mole sadly.

But Hare didn't tell his wife and friends what had happened, he felt too ashamed.

'What was the fight like?' asked Mrs Hare when he arrived home.

'Fine!' said Hare. 'Fantastic! Oh yes, a marvellous fight.'

'Who won?' said Mrs Hare.

'Fox of course. He chopped Badger into little pieces. Badger didn't even see him.'

Hare told the same story to all his friends, adding more to it and making it more exciting each time he told it, until, after he had told the tale half a dozen times, he believed it himself.

The other creatures told similar stories about the fight that never was to *their* friends and relatives. Some had it that Fox had won and some that the winner had been Badger. All made it sound as though it had been the most exciting fight that anyone had ever seen. The fight became a legend throughout the wood; sorry indeed were those creatures who had not been to Grasshopper Glade to see it. Some of them went to see Stoat and Weasel to see if they would put on another fight. Stoat smiled to himself his crafty smile and Weasel grinned his sly grin and they promised that one day they would put on another fight.

Fox and Badger still heard nothing about the fight. Everyone was afraid to speak to two such terrible fighters and they avoided them. But Fox did sometimes wonder why once, when he had returned home empty handed after visiting a farm to inspect some chickens, a basket containing a pair of fine fat ducks, roasted and ready to eat, and a bottle of champagne, was standing on the doorstep for him. And Badger, too, sometimes thought of the bag which held five pork pies and ten bottles of beer that he had found on his kitchen table when he had woken up from one of his long sleeps.

Which goes to prove that though most creatures are foolish none are all bad – not even Stoat and Weasel.

Vain Leopard

One day Leopard was out for a stroll. He walked proudly for he knew he was the most handsome beast in all the jungle. He came to a pool of clear water and looked down into it. Staring up at him was a face.

'A leopardess,' said Leopard. 'A beautiful leopard-

ess. She is as beautiful, or almost as beautiful, as I am myself.'

He grinned down at the leopardess and the leopardess grinned back.

He waggled his whiskers and the leopardess waggled *her* whiskers.

He stretched out his paw and showed the leopardess his sharp claws. She showed him *her* sharp claws.

'She has great spirit,' said Leopard. 'As great, or almost as great, as I have myself. I love her. I will go down and tell her how much I love her.'

He opened his jaws and gave a roar. The leopardess also opened *her* jaws and roared. The noise shook the jungle. Leopard was beside himself with love. He jumped down into the pool to show the leopardess how much he loved her and fell right into her great mouth which swallowed him up. Neither of them was ever seen again.

The Land on the Other Side of the Mountain

'I am tired of living here,' said Bear to his friend Buffalo.

'So am I,' said Buffalo. 'I think I will travel to the Land on the Other Side of the Mountain and try my luck there.'

'So will I,' said Bear. 'We will travel together.'

And so the two friends set out on their long journey to the Land on the Other Side of the Mountain. All went well until they came to the foot of the mountain and then they couldn't decide which way to go.

'We will climb straight up the mountain,' said Bear, 'and then down the other side.'

'No,' said Buffalo. 'We will go through the forest and round the mountain.'

'Over the mountain will be nearer,' said Bear.

'Through the forest will be quicker,' said Buffalo.

'Nonsense,' said Bear. 'The trees are so dense in places that we shouldn't be able to get through. We would be held up for days. Besides it is dangerous in the forest. There are deep swamps and all kinds of wild beasts.'

'It is not as dangerous as on the mountain,' said Buffalo. 'If we slipped there we could break our necks. In places the mountain is too steep to climb, we should never be able to get up. And at night it is so bitterly cold we could freeze to death.'

'We will go over the mountain,' said Bear, determined.

'We will go through the forest,' said Buffalo, equally determined.

'You're a fool,' said Bear.

'You're an idiot,' said Buffalo.

They glared at one another. Bear stood ready to strike Buffalo. Buffalo prepared to charge Bear.

'I am going over the mountain,' growled Bear.

'And I am going through the forest,' yelled Buffalo.

'I shall get there first.'

'Over my dead body,' said Buffalo. 'I shall get there long before you.'

They parted, now bitter enemies, and went their separate ways.

The way over the mountain was hard. The rocks were sharp and soon Bear's paws were cut and bleeding. Some parts were too steep for him to climb and he had to go back and find other ways. During the day the sun shone fiercely and Bear was hot. At night the mountain was cold and he lay and shivered, unable to sleep. 'I wish I'd gone with Buffalo,' he said, his teeth chattering. 'It must be easier travelling through the forest than climbing over the mountain.'

Meanwhile, Buffalo was also finding his journey hard. The forest was dense and it was difficult to push his way through. In many places the trees were so close together that it was impossible to get through at all. There were swamps too. He had to go farther and farther into the forest to avoid them until, after many days travelling, he was farther away from the Land on the Other Side of the Mountain than before he started out. The nights in the forest were frightening. Buffalo was terrified by the strange noises of the birds, beasts and reptiles. 'How wise Bear was, going over the mountain,' he said, trembling with fear. 'How I wish I had gone with him.'

Meanwhile Bear had climbed to the top of the high mountain. All he had to do now, to complete his long journey, was to climb down the other side. But this wasn't easy. Bear was desperately tired for he had been climbing for several days. He was also hungry for there was nothing to eat on the mountain. He shuffled and stumbled down. Many times he fell and was lucky not to break his bones. He was sure that Buffalo had arrived at the Land on the Other Side of the Mountain long ago and he wished he had gone with him.

Buffalo had travelled a great many miles, away

from the mountain, avoiding the swamps and the dense parts of the forest, but now he was on the last stage of his journey. He had long given up the race, for he was sure that Bear was already at the Land on the Other Side of the Mountain. At last, tired and sick, for he had been bitten by many insects and reptiles, Buffalo arrived at his destination, the Land on the Other Side of the Mountain. He stopped to have a drink at a pool. When he had drunk his fill he looked up to find that Bear was on the other side, also drinking at the pool.

'Bear,' said Buffalo, 'you have won the race for I have only just arrived.'

'No, I haven't,' said Bear. 'I have only just arrived too.'

'The journey through the forest was hard,' said Buffalo.

'No harder than the journey over the mountain,' said Bear.

They looked sadly at one another for a long time.

'It was stupid of us to quarrel,' said Bear.

'Yes,' agreed Buffalo. 'Both ways were equally hard. It didn't really matter which one we chose.'

'You are right,' said Bear. He looked round him. 'I am pleased I came here,' he said.

'So am I,' said Buffalo. 'It's a beautiful land and worth all the hardships of the journey.'

They set off together to explore their new land.

Mr and Mrs Wolf

'You're late, Mr Wolf,' said Mrs Wolf. 'What have you brought home?'

Wolf laid a chicken at Mrs Wolf's feet.

'A chicken! A chicken! You've been out all this time and all you've managed to catch is a chicken,' said Mrs Wolf. 'We had two chickens last week and three the week before. It's not good enough, Mr Wolf. It's not good enough.'

Wolf said nothing.

Mrs Wolf picked up the chicken and looked at it contemptuously. 'What's the matter with it? It's only got one leg. Why have you brought home a chicken with only one leg?'

'Well you see, Mrs Wolf,' said Wolf apologetically, 'I was just on my way home with the chicken when Lynx came along and tried to take it from me. He grabbed the leg of the chicken and ... and ...'

'And tore it off and ate it,' interrupted Mrs Wolf. 'The best part of the chicken and you allowed Lynx to eat it.'

'No it wasn't like that. You see ...'

'I don't want any of your excuses,' said Mrs Wolf. 'The leg of chicken that Lynx ate was your supper. You will get nothing else. It serves you right for being so weak and so stupid.'

Wolf said nothing. But inside his head he said to himself: 'One of these days, Mrs Wolf, I shall eat you. Just you see if I don't. I shall eat you.' Then he went to bed with no supper.

Mrs Wolf complained to Wolf about anything and everything he did. If he brought home too little she said she had hunger pains; if he brought too much she said she had indigestion. If he brought an animal she said the fur stuck in her teeth; if a bird the feathers got up her nose; if a fish the bones stuck in her throat. Nothing he did was right. If he went out she complained. If he stayed in she complained. If he lay in the sun she complained. If he ran about she complained. She blamed him for everything. She blamed him for the wind and the rain, and the sleet and the snow. She blamed him when it was dark and she had to go to bed; and when it was light and she had to get up. Nag, nag, nag, nag, nag from morning till night.

Wolf said nothing. But inside his head he always said: 'One of these days, Mrs Wolf, I shall eat you. Just you see if I don't. I shall eat you.'

One day Wolf was out hunting when, standing in the river, he saw Bear catching fish and eating them. He lay down behind a rock and watched. Bear caught a large silver fish. The sun glinted and gleamed on the fish's fat belly. It was a salmon. Wolf ran into the river and attacked Bear. He snatched the fish from his jaws. Bear was angry. How dare impudent Wolf attack him, mighty Bear! He struck a powerful blow with his huge paw on Wolf's nose. Wolf wanted to howl with pain but he didn't. He held the salmon tightly in his jaws and ran away with it. Bear ran after him.

Wolf could run faster than Bear and he lost him in the forest. Bear went back to catch some more fish. Wolf lay down to rest. His nose was bleeding from the terrible blow from Bear's claws. Sharp tears came to his eyes from the pain. But he was pleased. He had got the salmon; and what a fine, fat salmon. He had never eaten salmon before and neither had Mrs Wolf. How pleased she would be when she saw it. Proudly he carried it home.

Wolf laid the salmon at Mrs Wolf's feet.

'What,' said Mrs Wolf, 'is that?'

'It's a salmon,' said Wolf. 'The most delicious fish in the river. I fought Bear for it. Look what he did to me.' He showed Mrs Wolf the cut on his nose but she didn't look. She was looking at the salmon.

'What,' she said, 'is the matter with it?'

'What do you mean, dear?' said Wolf, puzzled.

'It's got no head. What have you done with the head?'

'Oh!' said Wolf. 'I hadn't noticed. Bear must have bitten it off.'

Mrs Wolf sniffed. 'What is the good of a fish without a head?'

'It doesn't matter,' said Wolf, 'the rest of it is perfectly all right ...'

'It is not all right,' cried Mrs Wolf. 'I will not have it here. Take it away.'

Wolf was angry, but he said nothing. He just lay

down to rest, his nose smarting from Bear's sharp claws. But inside his head he said: 'One of these days, Mrs Wolf, I shall eat you. Just you see if I don't. I shall eat you.'

'Didn't you hear what I said?' yelled Mrs Wolf in a rage. 'Get rid of that stinking fish. I will not have it.' She picked up the salmon and threw it at Wolf. 'Get out, and take that ... that thing with you.'

The salmon hit poor Wolf on the nose, making it smart worse than ever. He jumped up in pain. 'Right,' he said. 'You've asked for it, Mrs Wolf. You've asked for it,' and, before the startled Mrs Wolf could say anything, he leapt on her, caught her in his jaws, gave a mighty swallow – *gulp* – and devoured her.

At last Wolf could get a bit of peace. He lay down but he couldn't sleep for he had a pain in his stomach; Mrs Wolf was giving him indigestion. When he got up the next morning he still had the pain. 'It must be hunger,' he said. 'I'll have something to eat.' He ate the salmon and licked his chops. 'Delicious!' But the pain didn't stop. It grew worse. 'I'll lie still and quiet until it goes away,' he said to himself.

Suddenly Wolf pricked up his ears. He could hear something. A voice:

'Why did you eat that fish?'

What was that?

'That fish,' said the voice again, 'I said I would not have it.'

There was no mistake, Mrs Wolf was nagging him from inside his stomach. Poor Wolf, he gave a howl and rushed out. He ran into the forest. This way and that he ran, but he couldn't get away from Mrs Wolf's nagging voice: 'You're a fool, Mr Wolf. You're idle. You're weak. Stupid. Stupid. Weak. Idle. A fool, a fool, fool, fool, fool, foool, FOOOOOOLLL,' and she set up such a howling inside him that poor Wolf's body began to vibrate like a drum.

Wolf ran until he was tired and he lay down for a rest. Mrs Wolf still howled and nagged at him. He ran again, on and on and on he ran. At last he came to a river and could run no farther. He fell down on the bank exhausted. 'How tired I am,' he said. 'I must get some sleep.' He gave a mighty yawn and out of his mouth jumped Mrs Wolf. She dropped into the river with a plop and a howl and sank to the bottom.

Wolf fell into a deep, deep sleep.

When he awoke Wolf felt refreshed. Yes, he stretched out all his limbs, he definitely felt refreshed. He leaned over to the river and took some long gulps of water. He had never felt better in his life. He stopped; held his head on one side. What was that?

Gurgle, gurgle from the river, 'You're a fool, Mr Wolf, a fool, a fool, a fool, a fool, a foool-fooool-fooooool-FOOOOOOLLL.' Gurgle, gurgle, and bubbles came up from the bottom.

Oh no! She was nagging him again. She couldn't. But she did. Again the voice of Mrs Wolf came from the river:

'You're idle, stupid, weak. A fool, a fool, foool-fooool-foooool-fooooool-fooooooolll.'

Mr Wolf put his tail between his legs and ran.

Gradually, Wolf forgot about his wife. He began

to enjoy himself. He ate what he liked and when he liked. When he wanted fish he would eat fish and when he wanted chicken he would eat chicken. Some days he wasn't hungry and then he didn't bother to hunt for food, he just lay in the warm sun and snoozed, and there was no one to nag him and spoil his contentment.

Occasionally, very occasionally (usually when Wolf was feeling particularly happy), he would hear a voice. 'You're a fool, Mr Wolf,' it said. 'A fool, a fool, a fool, a fool – fooool – foooool – foooooll.' It was the voice of Mrs Wolf. Sometimes the voice came up from the river when Wolf was taking a drink; at other times it just seemed to come from inside his head. Luckily the voice came from a long, long way away. And in the end it came from so far away that Wolf couldn't hear it at all – even when he tried very hard.

The story of Goat and Leopard

One day Goat and Leopard met in the forest. Goat was feeling happy for he had gorged himself on the tender leaves of some young bushes. Leopard was feeling equally pleased for he had just eaten the best part of a water-buffalo which he had come upon by accident drinking in a forest pool. And so Goat and Leopard stopped to have a friendly chat.

'You know, Leopard,' said Goat, 'I would be your friend, but – I'm sure you don't mind me being frank – you frighten me. If I lay down beside you I would never be sure that one day you might not – in a fit of temper perhaps – jump upon me and tear me in pieces with those terrible sharp claws of yours.'

'Why, Goat, dear Goat,' said Leopard in his most soothing voice, 'I would never do that to you. Never. We can be good friends I assure you.'

'Nevertheless,' said Goat, 'I would feel happier if you were to cut your claws.'

'There is no need, dear Goat,' said Leopard, 'but, if it will make you feel any happier, I will certainly cut my claws,' and he went into the deep part of the forest and cut his claws. But, just to be on the safe side, he only cut the front claws – the back ones remained as sharp as ever.

'There you are, Goat,' said Leopard, showing him

his front claws. 'How does that suit you?'

'Oh that is much better,' said Goat. 'It really is decent of you, Leopard. We can now be friends.'

'Good,' said Leopard. 'I'm very glad.' Then, doubtfully, he said, 'There is just one thing Goat – I'm sure you don't mind me mentioning it – those horns of yours, they are formidable weapons. I wonder, dear chap, whether you would mind cutting off the sharp points, just for me?'

'Why there is no need for you to be afraid of my little horns,' said Goat, 'but, just for you, I will cut off the points,' and he went into the deep part of the forest and cut them off. But, just to be on the safe side, he hollowed them out and made them into a pair of sharp spikes which he could fit on to the stumps of the horns at any time he thought they might be necessary.

'Oh yes,' said Leopard when he had examined Goat's blunt horns, 'that is much better. Thank you, Goat. Now we can be friends.'

And so Goat and Leopard became friends. But neither trusted the other.

One day Goat said to Leopard, 'Do you know Leopard, it's very silly of me I know, but those teeth of yours are very sharp. I can't help wondering what would happen if you were to sink them into my soft flesh – not that you would ever dream of doing such a thing of course – but I wonder ... would you mind filing them down a little?'

'There is no need at all for you to be afraid, dear Goat,' said Leopard. 'I would never dream of hurting

you but, if it will make you feel happier, I will file down my teeth,' and he went into the deep part of the forest and filed down his teeth.

'There you are, Goat,' said Leopard showing him his blunt teeth, 'how does that suit you?'

'Oh that is much better,' said Goat. 'It really is decent of you. We can now be even closer friends.'

But, just to be on the safe side and unknown to Goat, Leopard began to go into the forest and practise crushing tree branches with his blunt teeth and soon he found they were just as dangerous as they had been when they were sharp.

One day Leopard said, 'You have very strong hind legs, Goat and very hard hooves, and – although I know you would never dream of doing so – you could easily kick in my ribs if you wished.'

'I would never do such a thing,' said Goat.

'I know you wouldn't,' said Leopard, 'but I wonder dear chap whether you would mind cutting off your hard hooves, just for me?'

'Why of course,' said Goat and he went into the deep part of the forest and cut off the hard hooves on his back feet.

'Oh yes that is much better,' said Leopard when he saw them. But, just to be on the safe side and unknown to Leopard, Goat practised kicking with his front feet and soon he could kick just as hard with them as he could with his back ones.

And so Goat and Leopard became even closer friends, but still they didn't trust one another.

One day Goat said to Leopard, 'What a terrifying roar you have, Leopard. I wish you wouldn't do it old chap. Eat grass like me and that will soften your voice.'

Leopard pretended to eat grass to please Goat, but when he was deep in the forest miles away from Goat he practised his roar till it was more terrifying than ever.

'I hardly like to mention it,' said Leopard to Goat one day, 'but you have a very bad temper, my dear fellow. You might do a mischief to someone one day. Milk, that's the thing. Drink milk and it will make you gentle.'

Goat pretended to drink milk just to satisfy Leopard and he was always sweet-tempered when Leopard was around, but secretly he remained just as fierce as ever.

Still Goat and Leopard distrusted one another.

One day Leopard said he was going to the far side of the forest to hunt. He set off early in the morning, but he didn't go to the far side of the forest. Instead he waited in the long grass until Goat came out to eat his breakfast of leaves and he followed him. He saw Goat put the pair of sharp spikes on his horns. He saw him practising fierce charges at the trees, tearing off great lumps of bark with the spikes. He saw him kicking the trees with his front hooves, until, in his temper, he made the trees shake, terrifying the poor monkeys and birds sheltering in their branches.

'The villain,' said Leopard to himself, 'I knew he wasn't to be trusted,' and he gave out such a terrifying roar that all the birds and beasts fell silent and Goat trembled with fear.

'How dare you!' yelled Leopard. 'I trusted you and this is what you do, practise your tricks behind my back. You wanted to be my friend you said, and all the time you were planning to kill me. Well I was ready for you, and now I am going to kill you.' He gave another terrifying roar and leapt at Goat.

But Goat had now got back his courage. He lightly stepped out of Leopard's way and then he charged at him. Leopard was taken by surprise and Goat tore off lumps of his beautiful coat with the sharp spikes. Leopard picked himself up. 'You crafty beast!' he snarled. 'Coming at me when my back was turned. I'll teach you a lesson,' and he hurled himself at Goat who caught one of his back legs in his jaws and bit it down to the bone.

And so began one of the most terrible battles ever seen in the forest. Birds and beasts came from miles around to see it. Goat and Leopard fought long and hard with all their courage. First one would be winning and then the other. Goat put out one of Leopard's eyes with his sharp spikes, making him shriek with pain; Leopard tore off both Goat's ears with his back claws; Goat rammed his horns into Leopard's side and broke three of his ribs. Neither could win the fight; neither would give in. The sun went down and the forest was in darkness. All the birds and beasts went to sleep. Goat and Leopard fought on in grim silence. They grew more and more weak, but still they fought. The sun rose. The chattering of the monkeys and the cries of the birds broke the silence. Goat and Leopard could fight no more and they fell down exhausted. They were in a terrible state. Leopard was blind in one eye, several of his ribs were broken and his beautiful coat was torn and coated with blood. Goat had a crushed foot and a broken leg, his ears were torn off and his white coat was also red with blood. They lay still as death.

The sun went down. Once more the forest was silent. It began to rain. Leopard stretched his limbs and winced with pain.

'Are you there, Goat?'

'Yes,' groaned Goat.

'You fought well.'

'You fought well yourself, Leopard.'

'I thought you were going to beat me at one time.'

'No, I could never beat you, Leopard. You fight much too hard.'

'I must go into the forest out of this terrible rain,' said Leopard.

'I will come with you,' said Goat. He tried to get to his feet but fell back again in pain.

'What's the matter Goat?'

'It's my leg, it's broken.'

'Come, I'll help you,' said Leopard. He helped Goat to get up and they hobbled away together deep into the forest to recover from their wounds.

Eventually Goat and Leopard's wounds healed. Goat was able once more to wander the forest in search of tasty young leaves, but now he walked with a limp for the leg that was broken didn't set properly, it was crooked and shorter than the others. Once again Leopard was able to hunt the animals of the forest, but many of them got away for he could not see them properly with only one eye.

But there is a happy ending to this sad story for Goat and Leopard became real friends. They were always together except when hunting for food. The beasts of the forest said they had never known two dearer friends. They would lie together, basking in the hot sun or sheltering from the pouring rain for many hours at a time. Sometimes they would talk, but usually they were silent, content just to be in one another's company, loving and trusting one another.

'We were very foolish having that fight, Leopard,' Goat would sometimes say.

'Yes,' Leopard would reply, 'very foolish. I should have trusted you, Goat and then it wouldn't have happened.'

'And I should have trusted you, Leopard.'

And the two friends would sigh, turn over and go to sleep.

Jenny Wren

Wren built a nest in the spring and showed it to his wife, Jenny.

'It is time you laid your eggs,' said Wren.

'I will not lay them yet,' said Jenny. 'The nest is not good enough. It needs fixing more firmly into the bush, otherwise when the wind comes it might blow away and, when I am sitting on the eggs, I shall get hurt.'

Wren fixed the nest more firmly into the bush.

'It is time you laid your eggs,' said Wren.

'I will not lay them yet,' said Jenny. 'The nest is not good enough. It needs more moss at the back and on top, otherwise when the rain comes it will rain in, and when I am sitting on the eggs I shall get wet.'

Wren fetched more moss and he put it on the back and the top of the nest.

'It is time you laid your eggs,' said Wren.

'I will not lay them yet,' said Jenny. 'The nest is not good enough. It needs lining with more soft down from your breast to make it cosy, otherwise when I am sitting for hours and hours on the eggs I shall be uncomfortable.'

Wren plucked more soft down from his breast and he lined the nest with it.

'It is time you laid your eggs,' said Wren.

'I will not lay them yet,' said Jenny. 'The nest is not good enough. It needs ...'

But Wren didn't hear what the nest needed. He had become tired of Jenny's excuses and had flown away.

Jenny Wren sat inside her nest and looked all round. It was perfect – or almost perfect (nothing could be perfect for her). It was so strong, proof against the wind and the rain; and so comfortable, she sank into the soft down which thickly lined it. Her little heart beat with pride.

But as the spring passed into summer unhappiness

crept into Jenny's heart. All the other birds had chicks, but she had none. The chicks learned to fly and some mother birds even had another brood. Still Jenny had none. She became deeply sad. She had no babies to love and to love her. She had only her beautiful nest.

She went in search of Wren and discovered that he had built another nest and had found himself another mate. They had their own chicks and Wren was proudly feeding them when she saw him. She went back to her own beautiful nest.

Summer passed away and autumn came. Jenny Wren wondered whether the winter would be hard and whether she would still be alive next spring to rear a brood of chicks, or whether she had missed her last chance. She grew lonely and miserable. She lost interest in her nest and couldn't think why she had been so proud of it. It was vanity. Just silly vanity.

The apes on the hill

Chump Chimpanzee was given his nickname because of his singing. At least Chump called it singing but the other apes didn't agree with him. Each time Chump opened his mouth to let out his *owooo-owooo-owoooooo*, which *he* regarded as singing, the other apes would groan and shout: 'What a noise! What a din! What caterwauling!' They even threw things at Chump to try and stop him but without success. *He* thought his singing was beautiful, and that the other apes were ignorant and stupid, and he carried on singing *owooo-owooo-owoooooo* until the others thought they would go mad if he didn't stop.

Barmy Baboon was given *his* nickname because of his poetry. At least Barmy called it poetry but the other apes didn't agree with him. When he recited his only poem, which consisted of one line, *Behold: beauty, beauty!* the other apes would groan and shout: 'What piffle! What rubbish! What gobbledegook!' They even threw things at Barmy to try and stop him but without success. *He* thought his poetry was beautiful and that the other apes were ignorant and stupid and he carried on reciting *Behold: beauty, beauty! Behold: beauty, beauty! Behold: beauty, beauty!* again and again and again, until the others thought they would go mad if he didn't stop.

Giddy Gibbon was given *his* nickname because of his acting. At least Giddy called it acting but the other apes didn't agree with him. He laughed to express joy, *ha-ha-ha*, cried to express sorrow, *boo-hoo-hoo* and beat his chest to express anger, *thump-thump-thump*. The other apes would groan and shout: 'What foolishness! What stupidity! What idiocy!' They even threw things at Giddy to try and stop him but without success. *He* thought his acting was beautiful and that the other apes were ignorant and stupid for not realizing it and he carried on acting *Ha-ha-ha, boo-hoo-hoo* and *thump-thump-thump* until the others thought they would go mad if he didn't stop.

Now Chump Chimpanzee, Barmy Baboon and Giddy Gibbon were friends. They liked each others' singing, reciting and acting, even though none of the other apes did. 'Bravo!' and 'Beautiful!' the two of them would shout when the third one was performing, and, 'Delightful!' and 'Divine!' and even – much to the annoyance of all the other apes – 'Encore!' (which means, 'We would like some more, please.').

Whether the three of them really did enjoy what their friends did, or whether they just pretended to like it in order to receive praise, it was difficult to say. Perhaps they didn't know themselves.

Sometimes the three apes gaves a concert. First Chump would sing, then Barmy would recite and then Giddy would act. Then they would all perform together. It sounded something like this: *owoooooo*

63

... behold ... ha-ha-ha ... owoooooo ... beauty ... boo-hoo-hoo ... owoooooo ... beauty ... thump-thump-thump. In order to make himself heard above the others Chump would sing louder. This just made Barmy recite louder and Giddy act louder. This meant that Chump had to sing louder still and Barmy recite louder still and Giddy act louder still, and so on and so on ...

Although the three friends enjoyed themselves the other apes were driven almost insane by the concerts. They shouted rude remarks in an attempt to make them shut up but were unable to make themselves heard above the noise. They put their hands over their ears to try and shut out the din but without success. Finally they begged them to stop. 'Please, please,

please,' they said. But Chump, Barmy and Giddy didn't hear them. They just carried on until they were too tired to go on any longer and then they stopped.

The apes all agreed that something had to be done about Chump, Barmy and Giddy. A meeting of the Ape Council was called to try and decide how they could be stopped from singing, reciting and acting. Some of the apes were all for sending them away. Some even thought they should be gagged. But the others thought that these answers to the problem were cruel. 'After all,' said King Gorilla, the leader of the council, 'we are civilized apes and civilized apes just don't do that sort of thing.'

They discussed the matter all day and all night without arriving at a solution. In the end it was decided that Chump, Barmy and Giddy should be asked, very politely, that is if they didn't mind, not to give any more performances of their singing, reciting and acting.

King Gorilla went to see them and put the apes' request to them. They were very annoyed. They said that they couldn't understand why the other apes didn't enjoy their singing, reciting and acting and that they had no intention of stopping the concerts, whether the apes enjoyed them or not. In fact they said that they would give more and more of them.

'Oh dear! Oh dear!' said King Gorilla. 'What shall we do? Perhaps you could think of a solution to the problem yourselves. If you could only go away somewhere perhaps and give your ... your ... concerts. Or perhaps if you could give them somewhere where they didn't sound quite so ... so loud. Or ... or ...'

'There is Tusk Hill,' said Giddy. 'We could give our concerts up there.' Tusk Hill was a high rock which pointed up to the sky like an elephant's tusk.

'What an excellent idea,' said King Gorilla. 'You could make your home up there and then you could sing, recite and act to your hearts' content. You could even give concerts all day and all night if you wished and no one would interfere with you or ask you to stop.'

'It is a very good idea,' said Barmy. 'But what would we live on? There is no food on Tusk Hill.'

'You could come down once a day and collect food,' said King Gorilla.

'No,' said Chump. 'Climbing up and down the hill would be exhausting. I would be too tired to sing after coming down, collecting food, and then going back again.'

'And I would be too tired to recite,' said Barmy.

'And I to act,' said Giddy.

'Oh dear! Oh dear!' said King Gorilla. 'And I thought we had found the perfect answer to our ...'

'Of course the other apes could collect food for us,' said Chump.

'And bring it up the hill,' said Barmy.

'Every day,' said Giddy.

'Mmmmmm,' said King Gorilla. 'I will have to ask the Ape Council.'

The members of the Ape Council were angry when they heard what Chump, Barmy and Giddy had proposed. 'They actually want us to collect food and take it up Tusk Hill for them whilst they do their idiotic singing, reciting and acting!' said a mandrill. 'The idea is preposterous.'

'It's either that or we shall have to put up with their infernal din for ever more,' said an orang-utan, looking gloomily across at the mandrill. 'The sound of Chump Chimpanzee's singing goes right through me; Barmy Baboon's poem is beginning to drive me insane; and as for Giddy Gibbon's acting ...'

The big orang-utan began to tremble violently, overcome with emotion, and was quite unable to say what he thought of Giddy's acting. King Gorilla had to go and place a comforting arm about his shoulders or he would have burst into tears.

'The orang-utan is quite right,' said one of the other apes, 'we must collect food for them. We cannot put up with any more of their terrible noise.'

There followed a long argument between those apes who agreed with the orang-utan and those who agreed with the mandrill. In the end they decided that anything would be better than having to listen any longer to Chump, Barmy and Giddy and so they agreed to collect food each day and take it up Tusk Hill for them.

And so Chump, Barmy and Giddy went to live on Tusk Hill. There they led a perfectly contented life. They got up late, ate and drank, lay in the sun, had little naps and sang, recited and acted just when they felt like it and nobody disturbed them. The other apes took turns at collecting food and water and taking it up the hill for them. They had no worries at all.

Sometimes, when the day was still and quiet, the apes would hear the sound of *owooo-owooo-owoooooo* drifting quietly on the breeze, or *behold: beauty, beauty!* or *ha-ha-ha, boo-hoo-hoo, thump-thump-thump*, and they knew that Chump, Barmy and Giddy were singing, reciting and acting, and they were grateful that they were far away on Tusk Hill.

Occasionally some other beast, Lion or Elephant or Hyena, would come along and, hearing the sounds coming from Tusk Hill and seeing the apes climbing up the hill with food, they would ask what was happening. The apes had a little tale which they told the other beasts on these occasions. 'Alas,' they would say, lowering their voices to a sad whisper, 'the apes up there are touched; lunatics. We keep them up the hill out of the way so that none of the rest of us is affected by them.'

'And you take all their food and water up to them?'

'Yes.'

'And they do nothing at all but make that dreadful noise?'

'Yes.'

The beast would then look up Tusk Hill to where Chump, Barmy and Giddy were enjoying their life of leisure, and then at the other apes who were kept busy feeding them, and he would walk away, shaking his head, as though not quite sure which of the apes were sane and which were lunatics.

At last, when Chump Chimpanzee, Barmy Baboon and Giddy Gibbon grew to be older and wiser, they came down from Tusk Hill, wearied of their life of idleness. The other apes welcomed them, for they also were tired of trudging up Tusk Hill every day with food.

Chump, Barmy and Giddy never gave any more concerts. They had sung, recited and acted so much that even they couldn't stand the noise any more. All the apes were pleased. None of them ever mentioned the matter again. It was just as though the concerts had never happened.

Hyena, the flatterer

'You are the strongest creature in the whole world,' said Hyena to Elephant one day when Elephant had taken hold of a large tree that blocked the path to the waterhole and had dragged it out of his way.

'Do you think so?' said Elephant, puffing a little from his efforts.

'Indeed,' said Hyena. 'There's no doubt about it. No one could have moved that heavy tree but you, Elephant.'

Elephant was very pleased by the praise and to show his pleasure he sucked up some water from the waterhole and sprayed it like a cool refreshing shower of rain over Hyena. Elephant proudly told everyone he met that he was the strongest creature in the whole world.

'You are the fastest creature in the whole world,' said Hyena to Cheetah one day when Cheetah had brought down a buck deer at full gallop and was now making a meal of it.

'Do you really think so?' said Cheetah, looking up from his feast.

'Certainly,' said Hyena. 'There's no doubt about it. No one could have caught that deer but you, Cheetah.'

Cheetah was very pleased by the praise and to show his pleasure he gave Hyena a tender joint off the dead deer. Cheetah proudly told everyone he met that he was the fastest creature in the whole world.

'You are the bravest creature in the whole world,' said Hyena to Lion one day when Lion had fought a ferocious battle with an angry water-buffalo and had beaten him.

'Do you really think so?' said Lion, tearing lumps of meat from the dead water-buffalo with his teeth.

'Indubitably,' said Hyena. 'There's no doubt about

it. No one could have fought and beaten a beast with such terrible horns as a water-buffalo but you, Lion.'

Lion was very pleased by the praise and to show his pleasure he made Hyena a present of the water-buffalo's horns. Lion proudly told everyone that he was the bravest beast in the whole world.

'You are the most humorous creature in the whole world,' said Hyena to Monkey one day when Monkey had had a whole collection of beasts falling about with laughter at his funny antics.

'Do you really think so?' said Monkey, hanging upside down from a tree by his tail.

'Absolutely,' said Hyena. 'There's no doubt about it. No one could have had all those creatures laughing like that but you, Monkey.'

Monkey was very pleased by the praise and to show his pleasure he did a comic dance followed by two dozen somersaults specially for Hyena. Monkey proudly told everyone that he was the most humorous creature in the whole world.

'You are the most handsome creature in the whole world,' said Hyena to Leopard one day as Leopard was admiring his reflection in a pool of water.

'Do you really think so?' said Leopard.

'Undeniably,' said Hyena. 'There's no doubt about it. No one has such a fine head, beautiful coat and grace of movement as you, dear Leopard.'

Leopard was very pleased by the praise and to show his pleasure he walked all round the pool so that Hyena could enjoy the sight of his beauty. Leopard proudly told everyone that he was the most handsome creature in the whole world.

One day Elephant, Cheetah, Lion, Monkey and Leopard met on the plain. They walked along together, chatting as they went. In the distance they saw Hyena.

'A fine fellow that Hyena,' said Elephant.

'Indeed yes,' they all said.

'Shrewd,' said Elephant.

'Perceptive,' said Cheetah.

'A good judge of courage,' said Lion.

'And of humour,' said Monkey.

'And beauty,' said Leopard.

'A really sound fellow,' all of them agreed.

By this time they were approaching Hyena and were going over to have a chat with him when they saw he was about to talk to Ostrich. That foolish bird had his head in the sand, hiding from Mouse who he thought was going to attack him and eat him. Hyena gave him a nudge to attract his attention and, when Ostrich took his trembling head out of the sand, he said to him:

'You are the wisest creature in the whole world, Ostrich.'

'Do you really think so?' said Ostrich, blinking sand from his eyes.

'Assuredly,' said Hyena. 'There's no doubt about it. No one is wise enough to realize that his enemies can't chase him down into the dark ground but you, Ostrich.'

Ostrich was very pleased by the praise, but Elephant, Cheetah, Lion, Monkey and Leopard who, unknown to Hyena, were listening nearby weren't pleased. They were angry with Hyena because they realized that if he could praise that most stupid of all creatures, Ostrich, for his wisdom then the praise he had bestowed on them must have been just empty flattery.

'You false wretch,' said Elephant. 'You have made fools of us all.'

'You must be punished,' said Lion and he and Cheetah and Leopard ran at Hyena and took hold of him. They were about to sink their sharp teeth into him and put an end to his miserable life, when Elephant said, 'Wait! Perhaps it was not entirely his fault. We were foolish to believe the flattering things he said about us so perhaps we were to blame just as much as Hyena. Let him go.'

They released Hyena. Then they told everyone they met how false Hyena was and how stupid they had been to believe everything he had said.

Soon all creatures knew that Hyena was a flatterer. Most took little notice whenever he praised them because they knew he was probably telling them lies.

Some still believed him, however. The vain, they believed him. They were always ready to believe anything he said to them, no matter how false or silly it might be just so long as it was nice, and with these creatures Hyena was always welcome.

Fox and Wolf

One day Fox met Wolf on the path. 'Good morning, Wolf!' he said with good humour. 'What a fine day it is. The sun is warm and yet there is a gentle breeze. It is good to be alive on such a day as this. Don't you agree?'

Wolf said nothing.

'Why don't you reply, Wolf?' said Fox. 'What is the matter with you?'

'I am depressed,' said Wolf. 'Depressed, miserable and sad.'

'And why are you depressed, miserable and sad?' asked Fox.

'For no reason,' said Wolf. 'It is how I was when I woke up this morning and how I shall remain for the rest of the day. If I were you I would go on your way Fox and leave me alone for I shall make poor company.'

'Nonsense,' said Fox. 'I will cheer you up. I know lots of funny stories, cheerful songs and all kinds of amusing tricks. We will walk along together and I will soon have you out of your unhappy mood.'

They walked along together and as they went Fox told Wolf all his funny stories; but Wolf didn't laugh. He sang him all his cheerful songs; but Wolf wasn't

cheered. He showed him all his amusing tricks; but Wolf wasn't amused.

At last Fox fell silent.

'What is the matter, Fox?' asked Wolf.

'I have caught your mood, Wolf,' replied Fox. 'I am depressed. Depressed, miserable and sad.'

They walked along a little way farther and then Wolf stopped. He stretched his limbs, then he said with good humour, 'What a fine day it is. The sun is warm and yet there is a gentle breeze. It is good to be alive on such a day as this. Don't you agree?'

Fox said nothing.

Wolf stretched his limbs again, yawned and twitched his whiskers, then he ran off into the wood.

'Wait,' said Fox. 'Aren't you going to keep me company?'

'Certainly not,' said Wolf. 'The last thing I want when I am feeling happy is to have a companion as depressed, miserable and sad as you,' and, with a flick of his tail, he vanished deep into the wood.

Leopard and Cheetah

Leopard was getting old and slow and was finding it difficult to hunt. He went to see his friend Cheetah. 'You are younger and faster than I, Cheetah, but I am bigger and stronger than you. Why don't we come to an arrangement? You do the chasing of prey and I will do the attacking and killing and we will share the meat between us.'

Cheetah thought the matter over. He *was* younger and faster than Leopard and was better at chasing prey. Leopard *was* bigger and stronger than he and better at attacking prey. It seemed a sensible plan.

'I agree,' said Cheetah. 'I will find prey and chase it and you will lie in wait and kill it. And we will share the meat equally between us.'

'Yes, we will share the meat equally between us,' agreed Leopard.

The arrangement worked well. Cheetah would go in search of prey and, when he found a succulent deer or zebra, he would chase it to where Leopard was lying in wait (usually up a tree for he was a fine climber). Leopard would jump on to the poor animal and kill it and then the two friends would share the meat between them.

But, like all such arrangements, it worked well only for a short time. One day Cheetah came upon a fine, fat gazelle – the biggest he had ever seen. He ran at it and chased it under the tree where Leopard was waiting. Leopard jumped down from the tree on to the gazelle, but he didn't kill it immediately. The gazelle put up a brave struggle and fought for its life. By the time he had managed to kill it Leopard was in a sorry state. There was blood on his beautiful coat where the gazelle had butted him with its horns, and his ribs ached from where it had kicked him.

When Cheetah came for his share of the gazelle, Leopard was annoyed. 'Why did you chase such a fierce animal?' he asked. 'Look how savagely it has attacked me.'

'I'm sorry, Leopard,' said Cheetah. 'I thought you would be more than a match for a mere gazelle, no matter how fierce.'

Leopard became angry. 'It seems to me that I am doing far more of the work than you, Cheetah. That gazelle almost killed me, whilst you are unmarked and aren't even out of breath. I should get far more of the meat than you as obviously my part of the work is harder and more dangerous.'

'I want an equal share of the gazelle,' said Cheetah. 'That was our bargain.'

'You shall have the hind legs only,' said Leopard, 'and that is more than you deserve.'

There followed a bitter quarrel. Cheetah rushed at Leopard to try and get his share of the gazelle, but he couldn't. Leopard was far too big and strong for him, and he had to run away into the jungle. When he returned some time later he found that Leopard had

dragged the gazelle up into a tree and he wouldn't give Cheetah any of the meat at all.

'I was willing to give you one of the hind legs,' said Leopard, 'which was more than you deserved. Now you shall have nothing. You can go hungry. Let that be a lesson to you for your ingratitude.'

'My ingratitude! My ingratitude!' said Cheetah. But then he could think of nothing else to say. The sheer effrontery of Leopard took away his power of speech. 'You ... you ... you cheat,' he said at last when it returned. 'I kept my side of the bargain but you didn't keep yours. You are the one that is ungrateful.'

'Go away, Cheetah,' said Leopard, chewing contentedly at his meat. 'You are beginning to annoy me.'

There was nothing Cheetah could do but go away. The tree was high and he was a poor climber. Besides, even if he had been capable of climbing the tree he would never have been able to take the meat from Leopard.

For two weeks Cheetah had nothing to eat but three frogs and a hare, which did little to satisfy his hunger. He was determined to get his revenge on Leopard but he couldn't think how. At last he thought of an idea. He went to see Leopard.

'Leopard,' he said, 'you were quite right about the gazelle. I was ungrateful – and greedy. I should have accepted what you offered me. I'm sorry.'

Leopard still occupied the high tree where he had eaten the gazelle. He was feeling happy with life; the gazelle had provided him with many meals. He looked down at the abject and hungry looking Cheetah.

'That's all right, old chap. You just got a bit above yourself that's all. It happens with you youngsters from time to time and we older beasts have to put you in your place. As long as you're sorry I'm willing to forget the whole thing.'

'That's very good of you, Leopard,' said Cheetah, choking back the angry words that came to his mouth. 'I am truly sorry for what I said. I was wondering,' he said, using his most humble tone of voice, 'if we could carry on with our arrangement. I will chase the prey and you can attack it and kill it.'

'Why certainly my dear Cheetah. There's nothing I'd like better. As long as you realize that attacking and killing the prey is much more difficult than just chasing it and therefore deserves more of the meat.'

'Yes of course, Leopard. You are absolutely right. I will go and find something for us and chase it this way. I will be as quick as I can for I am terribly hungry. As soon as you hear it coming you will jump down on it and kill it won't you?'

'All right, old friend,' said Leopard, stretching himself out on the branch of the tree. 'As soon as you're ready. Just chase it underneath and I will do the rest.'

Cheetah went back into the jungle to where, a little while before, he had seen Rhino browsing on some leaves.

'You are an ugly beast, Rhino,' said Cheetah when he had found Rhino. 'The ugliest beast in the whole of the jungle. Ugly! Ugly! Ugly!'

Rhino was a bad-tempered beast and normally he would have hurled himself at any creature foolish enough to call him names, but today he was feeling content with life. These leaves were delicious, so fresh and succulent. Soon he would have had enough of them and then he would go and have a pleasant snooze. 'Go away, Cheetah,' was all he said, and he said this in the gentlest of tones, as though he were speaking to one of his own children who had been mildly naughty.

Cheetah was determined to make Rhino lose his temper. He went nearer to him. 'You are a stupid beast, Rhino,' he said, 'the stupidest beast in the whole of the jungle. Stupid! Stupid! Stupid!'

'If you don't go away, Cheetah,' said Rhino patiently, 'I shall have to teach you a lesson.'

Cheetah went nearer to Rhino, barely a tail's length away. 'You are a ridiculous beast, Rhino,' he said. 'That horn of yours, stuck on the end of your nose like a shrivelled banana, it makes you look like a clown.'

Now there was one thing that Rhino would not tolerate, no matter how pleased with life he was, and that was any creature making fun of his horn. He would stand that from no one, not even Lion, Elephant or Hippo. As for this spotted pussy cat ... He would soon teach him to respect his betters and, without warning, he threw himself at Cheetah.

Luckily Cheetah was on his guard and he ran away. He ran towards the tree where Leopard was waiting and Rhino ran after him. Just before he got to the tree, Cheetah left the track and dived into some bushes, but Rhino went blundering on.

Up in his tree Leopard heard the noise of running feet and, thinking that Cheetah was chasing prey, he poised himself ready to spring. He jumped. Too late he saw that the prey, instead of being a frightened antelope or a plump young zebra, was Rhino, bad-tempered, angry Rhino, and he had landed on his back.

Rhino went berserk. He ran through bushes and pools and under low branches, and threw himself this way and that to try and dislodge Leopard. Leopard clung desperately to his thick skin, afraid of falling off in case he broke his neck. He was scratched, bruised and frightened.

At last, tired out by his efforts, Rhino slowed down and Leopard was able to jump off his back and scramble to safety up a tree.

Leopard stayed up the tree for ten days. Not until he was certain that Rhino was not lurking nearby was he brave enough to come down. By then he was very, very hungry.

Leopard made several attempts to catch prey himself but without success. He was so slow that even the youngest game could outrun him. Tired out he lay down to recover his strength. Cheetah came up and sat down beside him. He looked well-fed and content with life.

'What happened to you the other day?' Cheetah asked.

'What do you mean?' said Leopard.

'I found a plump young pig,' said Cheetah, 'and I chased it under the tree as we arranged so that you could kill it and when I got there I found you having a fight with Rhino. I had to kill the pig myself and eat it. It was delicious. You would have enjoyed it, Leopard. There's nothing like fresh pork – unless it's Rhino meat perhaps. Was that nice, Leopard? Rhino, was he nice to eat?'

Leopard looked up and saw Cheetah smiling slyly at him and he knew he had been tricked. If he had been younger he would have told the impudent beast just what he thought of him, and he'd have let him feel the sharpness of his claws and teeth too. But now he was too old and too tired. If he said anything to him Cheetah would only laugh, and if he tried to attack him he would just run away. So Leopard said nothing and did nothing.

Cheetah got up, stretched himself pleasurably, and yawned. 'I'll be going now, Leopard,' he said. 'I'll come and see you in a few days' time. Perhaps we can catch some game together,' and he walked slowly away.

Leopard seethed with anger but still he said nothing. He just lay still and tried to forget the hunger pains in his stomach.

The two friends made up their quarrel. They continued hunting together, Cheetah doing the chasing and Leopard the attacking and killing. Sometimes the chasing was easy and the killing was hard. At other times the chasing was hard and the killing easy. They accepted this and divided the meat equally between them. If Leopard ever tried to take more than his fair share Cheetah would mention that he had seen Rhino that day. 'He is looking for you, Leopard,' he would say. 'He says he wants a little chat with you about something. I said I didn't know where you were,' and Leopard would suddenly lose his appetite.

'Take as much meat as you like, Cheetah,' he would say. 'We older beasts do not need to eat as much as you younger ones,' and Cheetah would smile slyly to himself.

Occasionally, when he was feeling playful, Cheetah would run round and round Leopard and impudently nip his tail. He thought, just because he had once got the better of Leopard with his clever trick, that he could behave just as he wished. When this happened, Leopard would reveal his sharp claws, flex his muscles, and growl menacingly. Cheetah knew then that, if they ever fought, Leopard would be sure to win and he showed him the respect that was due to an older and larger beast. Cheetah was no fool.

Woodlouse and Ant

Woodlouse crawled from under the dark, damp tree, where he had been nibbling dead wood, and out into the sunshine. He wasn't used to the light; it was so bright that it almost blinded him. He had decided to go straight back under his cosy tree and chew some more dead wood when a very strange sight caught his eye. It was so strange that at first he couldn't believe it. The bank just in front of him was moving. It was turning one way and the other, and forwards, backwards and sideways, all at the same time. He had never seen anything like it before. He rubbed his eyes to make sure he wasn't dreaming.

Then one of the moving bits of bank ran over to him and said, 'Good morning, Woodlouse,' and he saw that it was Ant. He realized then that the moving bank was an ant colony. There were thousands and thousands of ants, all scurrying hither and thither, here and there, round and round, and in and out of the bank, never stopping for a single instant.

'My word it makes me dizzy to watch you ants,' said Woodlouse to Ant. 'Don't you ever stop?'

'Never,' said Ant, running round and round on the same spot. 'No time. Far too busy. Not a moment to waste.'

'But what do you do?' said Woodlouse. 'Always in

a frantic hurry. Never stopping for anything.'

'Do? Do?' said Ant. 'Everything. Build nests, guard the eggs, feed the grubs, find food, store it, tidy up the wood – debris, leaves, twigs, dead creatures. My dear Woodlouse we have plenty to do.'

'But why the hurry, Ant. We woodlice never hurry.'

'You have to hurry if you are going to succeed, Woodlouse. And we ants are going to succeed. We intend to take over the world.'

'Forgive my ignorance, Ant,' said Woodlouse. 'I live a quiet life with my friends under the dead trees, but would you mind telling me this: what is the world? And why do you wish to take it over?'

Ant was agitated by the question. He ran round and round at such speed that he began to wear a hole in the ground. 'Dear me! Dear me! Dear me!' he said. 'Why this is the world, Woodlouse, this wood, the ground, the sky, the oceans, the birds, beasts and fishes. Everything we know is the world. Everything. We wish to take it over because we are good at running things. We are efficient. We never waste a moment of time.'

'How dull my life is compared with yours, Ant,' said Woodlouse, sadly. 'All I ever do is chew dead wood. We woodlice have no ambition. We chew dead wood in the morning, the afternoon and the evening. And if we wake up in the middle of the night all we can think of doing to pass the time is to chew a bit more dead wood.'

'But that is a worthwhile task, Woodlouse,' said Ant. 'You eat the dead trees in order to clear the ground for new ones to grow. But you take too long about it, that is the trouble. You nibble away so slowly, it takes you years to dispose of a single tree. We ants would do it with urgency. We'd devour a tree in a single day and then start on another one the next. All the dead trees in the wood would be gone in no time at all.'

'Really?' said Woodlouse.

'Really!' said Ant. 'And now I must be going. I've enjoyed our little chat, Woodlouse, but I have lots to do. Work! That is the thing my dear chap. Work, work, work. You have to work hard if you intend to take over the world.' And, spinning round four times the one way and then five times the other, Ant set off at full speed back to his colony and was lost in the moving mass of ants.

Back under his dark, damp tree, quietly chewing dead wood, Woodlouse thought over what Ant had said. There was a lot of sense in it. Ants led a far more interesting life than woodlice. More purposeful. All that activity. Never stopping. 'I'll do the same,' he said. 'I'll be like the ants.' And without wasting any more time Woodlouse set to work. Instead of quietly chewing away at the dead wood he began to eat it the way the ants might have eaten it. He ran up and down under the dark, damp tree, breaking off lumps of dead wood and chewing them fast and furiously. The other woodlice watched him in amazement.

'What on earth are you doing?' one of them said.

'Eating this tree,' said Woodlouse.

'We can see that, but why are you in such a hurry?'

'You have to hurry if you are going to succeed,' said Woodlouse, 'and I am going to succeed. I intend to take over the world: this wood, the ground, the sky, the oceans, the birds, beasts and fishes.'

'Why?'

'Because ...' said Woodlouse. 'Because ... Oh I haven't got time to discuss the matter. I have far too much to do. Come and help me some of you.' And he ran backwards and forwards, from side to side, and round and round, gobbling up the dead wood as fast as he could.

The other woodlice ignored him. They just carried on chewing the wood at their usual slow speed.

After a few hours Woodlouse was exhausted, tired out. He used his last remaining strength to crawl from under the dark, damp tree. There his legs gave way beneath him and he lay gasping for breath, unable to move, in the sunshine.

The ant colony still surged in a pulsating mass upon the bank. Ant left the colony and came over to Woodlouse.

'What is the matter, Woodlouse?' he asked.

'I am done for,' groaned Woodlouse. 'I am incapable of working like you ants. I am dying.'

'Dying?' said Ant. 'Oh dear! Oh dear! Never mind, I think I can be of help, Woodlouse. Wait there and I will fetch some of my friends.'

'What will you do?' said Woodlouse.

'We will carry you back to our nest,' said Ant, 'and then we will chop you up into small pieces and feed you to our grubs.'

'Do you mean you are going to kill me?' said Woodlouse.

'Well you said yourself that you were dying. There's no point in wasting your body is there? We ants do not believe in waste. That's why we will take over the world. Just wait there Woodlouse, I'll be right back.'

Woodlouse thought he had used up all his strength but he still had a tiny bit left, just enough to drag himself back under the dark, damp tree.

When he had recovered, Woodlouse no longer

wanted to be like an ant, nor did he wish to take over the world. He was content to be like all the other woodlice and just nibble slowly at the dead wood. He rarely left the shelter of the dark, damp tree. Whenever he looked out and saw the ants he thought to himself, 'How stupid they are, scurrying about like mad things when they could take things nice and slowly. It makes me tired just to watch them,' and he would go back immediately under the dark, damp tree.

He had an idea too that Ant and his friends might be lurking just outside and he didn't fancy providing a meal for their grubs.

The two barnacles

Two barnacles clung to a rock. They didn't speak much. When they did it was very slowly.

One day the first barnacle said, 'It's dull here. If we were on a ship instead of this boring rock we could see the world.' The second barnacle said nothing.

The tide came in, gulping and splashing and gurgling, and covered the rock. The barnacles had to cling on tightly to avoid being washed off the rock.

'Are you coming with me?' said the first barnacle, when the tide had gone out.

'Where?' said the second.

Again the tide came gulping, splashing and gurgling in, covering the rock. Again it went out.

'On a ship to see the world,' said the first barnacle.

'Oh that,' said the second. 'I don't know. I haven't made up my mind.'

The tide came in again, gulping, splashing and gurgling over the rock. It went out.

'Well, have you decided?' said the first barnacle.

'I need a little more time to think about it,' said the second.

The tide gulped, splashed and gurgled over the rock once more, and once more it went out.

'I have made up my mind,' said the second barnacle.

'Good,' said the first. 'What have you decided?'

But he never found out because the tide came gulping, splashing and gurgling in, and with it came a large, fat whelk. It ate both of the barnacles.

The kite

Rabbit was nibbling his way through a field of dandelions when he came upon Fox. Fox was behaving in a very strange manner. He was pacing up and down, making marks on the ground and muttering to himself.

'What are you doing, Fox?' said Rabbit. Fox didn't hear him, for he was completely absorbed.

'Fox,' said Rabbit again, 'what are you doing?'

Fox stopped and turned round. 'Oh, it's you, Rabbit,' he said, annoyed at being interrupted. 'I can't tell you. It's a secret. But,' he added mysteriously, 'it's something marvellous, amazing and wonderful and it will make my fortune.' And, ignoring Rabbit, he carried on with his pacing, making marks on the ground, and muttering. Rabbit sat and watched Fox at his strange work.

Badger was in the wood making a meal of juicy grubs when he looked out over the field and saw Fox. He lumbered across to have a closer look.

'What's Fox doing?' said Badger to Rabbit.

'I don't know,' said Rabbit. 'But it's something marvellous, amazing and wonderful and it will make his fortune.' And they both sat and watched Fox at his strange work.

Mole was digging a long, dark tunnel under the

ground. Suddenly he broke through into the sunlight. He blinked and looked round. He saw Fox and strolled across to see what he was up to.

'What's Fox doing?' said Mole to Badger and Rabbit.

'I don't know,' said Badger. 'But it's something marvellous, amazing and wonderful and it will make his fortune.' And the three of them sat and watched Fox at his strange work.

Stoat was up a tree, eating the eggs in a blackbird's nest, when he saw Fox. He climbed down and crawled across the field to see what he was doing.

Hare was bounding along the hedgerow, chasing his own shadow, when he saw Fox. He changed direction and bounded across to see what he was doing.

Water-vole had been swimming all morning in the cool stream. He climbed out to dry in the warm sun when he saw Fox. He ambled across to see what he was doing.

'What's Fox doing?' said Stoat and Hare and Water-vole together.

'We don't know,' said Rabbit, Badger and Mole. 'But it's something marvellous, amazing and wonderful and it's going to make his fortune.' And they all sat and watched Fox at his strange work.

Fox stopped. He turned round and saw, with surprise, Rabbit, Badger, Mole, Stoat, Hare and Water-vole, watching him.

'Oh hello!' he said, but, before they could reply, he turned his gaze on to the strange marks he had made on the ground. 'Beautiful isn't it?' he said, proudly.

'What is it?' said the others.

'It's something marvellous, amazing and wonderful and it will make ...'

'We know all about that,' said the others impatiently, 'but what *is* it? What *is* it?'

'Can't you *see*,' said Fox. 'It's a drawing.'

'So it is,' said Rabbit. 'It's a drawing of a juicy carrot.'

'No it isn't,' said Badger. 'It's a huge grub.'

'A very large worm,' said Mole.

'A fine, fat pheasant,' grinned Stoat.

'A turnip,' said Hare.

'A boat with a sail,' said Water-vole.

'No it isn't,' said Fox angrily. 'It isn't any of those things. It's my very own original design for a kite. It's marvellous, amazing and ...'

'We know all that,' interrupted the others, rudely.

'... and it's going to make my fortune,' continued Fox.

'What will you use for the fabric?' asked Rabbit.

'It will be big. Bigger than Horse or Cow ...' went on Fox dreamily.

'What will you use for the frame?' asked Badger.

'... and it will sail high in the air, sporting with the clouds ...'

'How will you stick it together?' asked Mole.

'... it will swoop across the sky faster than Hawk ...'

'What will you use for the tail?' asked Stoat.

'... and more silent than Owl ...'

'What will you use to paint the design?' asked Hare.

'... animals will come from fields and hedgerows, woods and streams for miles and miles around to see it ...'

'What will you use for the string?' asked Water-vole.

'... and they will give me whatever I ask. It's going to be so exciting and ...'

'Will they give you juicy carrots?' said Rabbit.

'And huge grubs?' said Badger.

'Very large worms?' said Mole.

'Fine fat pheasants?' grinned Stoat.

'A turnip?' said Hare.

'A boat with a sail?' said Water-vole.

'Yes! Yes! Yes! Yes! Yes! Yes!' said Fox impatiently. 'Everything! They will bring me everything I want.'

'We will help you make this kite,' said the others.

Rabbit went away to a farm to collect some paper bags to make the kite's fabric. Badger went to a garden he knew to fetch some long canes to make the frame. Mole had once found a tube of glue which he had hidden in one of his tunnels and he went to fetch it so that they could stick the kite together. Stoat went deep into the wood to collect some pretty, coloured feathers to make the tail of the kite. He grinned slyly to himself and licked his chops when he thought of the birds that had once owned the feathers. Hare bounded away to a rubbish dump on the far side of the wood where he remembered seeing a child's paintbox which they could use to paint a design on the kite. And Water-vole dived back into the river and swam along the bank, collecting several fishing lines that were caught in the weeds to make the string and the tail of the kite.

They all set to work under Fox's supervision. They tied the canes together to make a frame; cut and stretched the paper and glued it on to the frame; tied a piece of fishing-line to the bottom with lots of pretty feathers on it to form a tail; painted a lovely pattern on the kite of blue and purple and green (these were the only colours in the paintbox); and then Fox lifted it up to make sure it was properly balanced.

'Perfect!' he said proudly. 'It's marvellous, amazing and wonderful.' He took one end of the fishing-line and tied it to the frame of the kite. 'Now,' he said, 'I am going to make it fly.'

'Wait a moment, Fox,' said Rabbit. 'You're forgetting the juicy carrots ...'

'... and the huge grubs ...'

'... and the very large worms ...'

'... and the fine fat pheasant ...'

'... and the turnip ...'

'... and the boat with a sail ...'

'We have worked very hard making the kite,' they all said, 'and now we want our reward.'

'Of course,' said Fox. 'I was forgetting. Well if you will all go to the fields, hedgerows, woods and streams and tell the animals, birds and reptiles you meet to come here and to bring with them juicy carrots ... and ... and ... and ... What else was it?'

'... huge grubs,' said Badger.

'... very large worms,' said Mole.

'... fine fat pheasants,' grinned Stoat.

'... turnips,' said Hare.

'... and a boat with a sail,' said Water-vole.

'Quite!' said Fox. 'Tell them all that and tell them they can see the most marvellous, amazing and wonderful ...'

But Fox was talking to himself. The others had already left.

The animals, birds and reptiles of the fields, hedge-rows, woods and streams, gathered at the edge of the field of dandelions and listened to Fox making a speech.

'You are about to see,' said Fox, 'the most marvellous, amazing and wonderful thing you have ever seen in your lives.'

As Fox was making his speech, Rabbit, Badger, Mole, Stoat, Hare and Water-vole were going round the crowd trying to persuade the animals, birds and reptiles to give up what they had brought with them.

'This kite,' continued Fox, 'this marvellous, amazing and wonderful kite which, as you can see, is bigger than Horse or Cow, is going to sail high in the air, sporting with the clouds ...'

'If I could just have your juicy carrots,' said Rabbit.

'... huge grubs,' said Badger.

'... very large worms,' said Mole.

'... fine fat pheasants,' grinned Stoat.

'... turnips,' said Hare.

'. . . boat with a sail,' said Water-vole.

'This marvellous, amazing and wonderful kite will swoop across the sky faster than Hawk and more silent than Owl,' said Fox.

'If we could just have your carrots, grubs, worms, pheasants, turnips and boat with a sail,' said Rabbit, Badger, Mole, Stoat, Hare and Water-vole, 'before Fox sends up the kite.'

'But how do we know the kite will work?' said the others. 'We want to see it go up and then we will give you our things.'

'You must give us your things first and then Fox will fly the kite.'

'No,' said the others. 'Fox must fly the kite and then we will give you the things.'

They began to quarrel. Rabbit, Badger, Mole, Stoat, Hare and Water-vole wouldn't allow the other creatures to see the kite go up until they had given them their things, and the others wouldn't give up their things until they saw whether the kite would fly.

'If you won't give up your juicy carrots . . .'

'. . . huge grubs,'

'. . . very large worms,'

'. . . fine fat pheasants,'

'. . . turnips,'

'. . . a boat with a sail,'

'. . . then you shan't see the kite.' And Rabbit, Badger, Mole, Stoat, Hare and Water-vole chased the creatures out of the field of dandelions.

Meanwhile Fox was still making his speech: 'And

now friends you are about to see the most marvellous, amazing and wonderful ... Oh!' he said, seeing that he was now on his own. 'They've all gone. Never mind, I'll carry on anyway,' and he held up the kite. A gust of wind immediately caught it and blew it high into the air, high, high, high over the treetops.

From the fields all round, the animals, birds and reptiles saw the kite flying up in the clouds and they were thrilled. 'Hurray!' they yelled, 'Hurray! Hurray! Hurray!' as the kite swooped across the sky, faster than Hawk and more silent than Owl. 'How stupid Rabbit and Badger and Mole and Stoat and Hare and Water-vole were,' they said, 'expecting us to pay to watch the kite from the dandelion field when we can see it for nothing from anywhere, anywhere at all.' And they laughed and laughed and laughed.

Rabbit, Badger, Mole, Stoat, Hare and Water-vole watched the kite too and they were thrilled. But they were hungry too for they hadn't eaten anything for a long time.

'How I would love a juicy carrot,' said Rabbit.

'... huge grubs,' said Badger.

'... very large worms,' said Mole.

'... a fine fat pheasant,' said Stoat.

'... turnips,' said Hare.

'... anything at all,' said Water-vole.

'How foolish we have all been,' they said, all together, and they made their way home, sadder and wiser animals.

The most thrilled of all the animals was Fox. He

had forgotten the hard work that had gone into making the kite and all those who had helped him to make it. He could think of nothing but how marvellous, amazing and wonderful the kite was. It hadn't made his fortune, but that didn't matter. All that mattered to him was the sheer joy of flying his kite and he went on flying it until long after the sun had gone down.

The man and the camel

A man was riding a camel through the desert. The sun blazed down and the man was hot. The camel was walking along at a nice, steady pace but this wasn't fast enough for the man. He was in a hurry to get to camp. He hit the camel with his stick to make it go faster. The camel lengthened its stride for a while but then it went back to its usual steady pace. The man hit the camel again and again but it made no difference. The camel travelled at its own speed. There was a sharp spike at the end of the stick and the man began to poke this into the camel's side. The camel didn't like this.

'Go faster,' said the man, 'or I'll poke you again.'
'No,' said the camel.

The man poked the camel again with the spike.

'If you do that again,' said the camel, 'I will throw you off my back and *you* shall carry *me*.'

'Don't be ridiculous,' said the man. 'I am a man and we men are mighty. We are able to bend all creatures to our will. You are just an ignorant camel. It is my right to hit you with my stick, and poke you with my spike if I wish, and it is your duty to carry me on your back and take me where I want to go,' and once more he poked the camel with his spike.

The camel stopped and, with a heave of his hump,

he threw the man to the ground, knocking all the wind out of him. The man got up and tried to climb back on to the camel, but the camel wouldn't let him. He knocked the man down again and, when the man tried to get up, the camel put one of his big feet on him so that the man couldn't move.

'Now, mighty man,' said the camel, '*you* shall carry *me*.'

'I refuse,' said the man. 'A noble man will not carry an ignoble camel.'

'Then you shall stay on the ground until you starve,' said the camel, 'and the birds and reptiles will come and pick your bones.'

The sun blazed down. There was sand in the man's hair and in his eyes and each grain of sand felt like a red hot ball of glass. The camel's foot was like a heavy rock upon the man's chest and he couldn't move. But the man was proud. He would not bend to the camel's will. Wasn't he a mighty man, and wasn't the camel just an ignorant camel?

The sun was right overhead. It hung in the sky like a ball of fire. A vulture, black and fearsome, hovered over the man and the man eyed it with terror. A scorpion, with poison in its tail, came from behind a rock and watched the man.

'I give up,' said the man. 'I will carry you,' and the camel allowed the man to get up.

The man was carrying the camel through the desert. The sun had moved across the sky but had lost none of its heat. It fiercely burned the man. Sweat ran down his face and into his eyes and his mouth.

The camel was heavy and the man walked slowly. Unlike the camel the man did not have big feet which could walk on top of the sand, and with every step he took the man sank into the sand up to his knees. Several times he stumbled and almost fell. His back ached with the effort of carrying the camel and he went slower and slower.

'I am uncomfortable,' said the camel.

'There is nothing I can do about that,' said the man. 'I am carrying you the only way I am able.'

'You could go faster,' said the camel, 'and then I wouldn't have to put up with the discomfort for very much longer.'

'I can't go any faster,' gasped the man.

'Yes you can,' said the camel, and he hit the man with the stick. The man tried to walk faster but he couldn't. The camel poked him with the spike. The man tried to run but he stumbled and fell.

The camel was angry. 'Mighty man!' he said, scornfully. 'You can't even walk through the desert without falling over, while I, an ignorant camel, can walk for days on the soft sand without getting tired and without needing food or water.'

Once more the man set off with the camel on his back. The sun was now low in the sky. Soon it would be dark.

'We shall be arriving in camp shortly,' said the camel. 'Your friends will come out and see you, a mighty man, carrying me, an ignorant camel. They will tell the story to everyone, and all men will know throughout the land. You will never dare to look your fellows in the eye again. They will laugh at you and say "There goes the man who carries his camel upon his back".'

The man wept tears of humiliation for he knew that what the camel said was true.

'But I do not wish you to carry me upon your back,' said the camel, 'because the other camels will laugh at me too when they see me being carried by a man, and I do not wish that to happen, for I also have my pride. I will make a bargain with you. I will carry you into camp and, from now on, I will take you wherever you wish to go, but you must never hit me with a stick again or poke me with a spike.'

The man agreed. The camel carried the man on his back into camp and from then on took him wherever he wished to go. They never quarrelled again. Occasionally the man felt impatient and wanted the camel to go faster but, whenever he felt tempted to hit the camel with a stick or poke him with a spike, he remembered the time when he had had to carry the camel through the hot desert, and he realized that he was not the mighty man he had once thought himself to be, and neither was the camel such an ignorant camel.

The blue snails

There were snails of many colours living in the big field; pink and white and blue; green, yellow, purple and brown; black, grey, orange and red. They lived all jumbled together, wandering happily about the field in their slow, snail-like way. From a distance the field of snails looked like a field of pretty coloured stones.

One day a blue snail was nibbling her way along a dock leaf when, half way along, she came upon another blue snail who was nibbling her way from the other end of the leaf. They stopped in the middle to have a chat. They chatted happily together for several minutes.

'How polite and agreeable this snail is,' thought the first snail of the second.

'How friendly and well-mannered,' thought the second snail of the first.

'Do you know,' said the first snail, 'we Blues are much better than the others.'

'Oh quite so,' said the second. 'More intelligent, more handsome, more imaginative, more refined.'

'How right you are. You are absolutely right. We are so much better than those awful Reds for example.'

'Indeed yes,' said the second snail. 'The Reds are loud-mouthed and vulgar.'

'I agree with you entirely. And if anything I think the Yellows are worse: feather-brained.'

'Weak in the head if you ask me,' said the second snail.

'And those Greens! So greedy,' said the first.

'And jealous,' said the second. 'They want everything that anyone else has.'

'And how about those dreadful Purples?' said the first snail.

'Snobs!' said the second snail. 'They think they're better than everyone else.'

'And what do you think of the Blacks?'

'Grumpy,' said the second snail. 'And those Greys are so terribly dreary.'

'Quite so. And the Browns are ugly,' said the first snail, 'and the Whites insipid.'

'The Pinks are brazen,' said the second snail, 'and the Oranges such conceited show-offs.'

'You are right. You are absolutely right,' said the first snail. 'I agree with every word you say. We Blues are better in every way than the others.'

'Better in every way,' agreed the second snail.

'I have an idea,' said the first snail. 'Why don't we Blues live together, away from the others.'

'Yes,' said the second snail. 'We could have a field of our own, or live in a separate enclosure, so that we didn't have to mix with the others at all.'

'Excellent,' chuckled the first snail. 'I knew you would agree with me.' And the two snails set off to tell all the other blue snails of the idea.

The blue snails all thought the idea was good and

they decided to put it into practice. They built a fence in one corner of the field so that they could live together away from the others. Now they were happy. They ate together and walked together and talked intelligently together. None of the other snails could interfere with them for *they* were on the other side of the fence.

One day some seagulls flew over the field of snails. They saw the strange blue patch in one corner and they wondered what it was. They glided down to find out. When they saw the blue snails they fell upon them greedily and ate them all up, every single one. But they didn't eat any of the others because they were still jumbled together and they thought they were just pretty coloured stones.

Rudyard Kipling
Just So Stories 70p

Did you know how the camel got his hump, the leopard his spots
or how the whale got his throat ? Rudyard Kipling can tell you in
what is perhaps the most famous of all his books.

Gail Robinson and Douglas Hill
Coyote the Trickster 95p

The Trickster is a magical creature, with special powers, who
appears in various disguises — coyote, raven, hare and fox.
He is foolish enough to get into trouble, but cunning enough to
get out of the difficulty.

A unique collection of stories from the rich legends and folk
tales of the North American Indians.

You can buy these and other Piccolo books from booksellers and
newsagents ; or direct from the following address :
Pan Books, Sales Office, Cavaye Place, London SW10 9PG
Send purchase price plus 25p for the first book and 10p for
each additional book, to allow for postage and packing
Prices quoted are applicable in the UK

While every effort is made to keep prices low, it is sometimes
necessary to increase prices at short notice. Pan Books reserve
the right to show on covers and charge new retail prices which
may differ from those advertised in the text or elsewhere